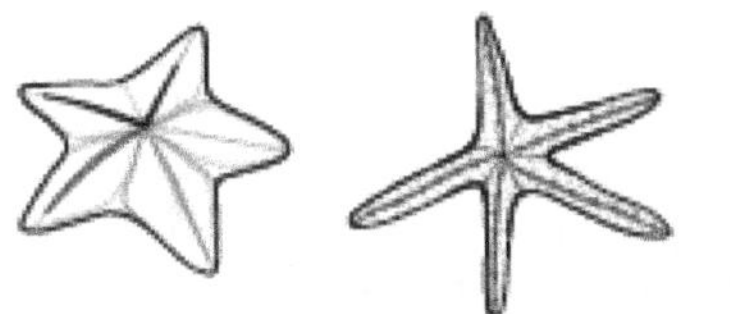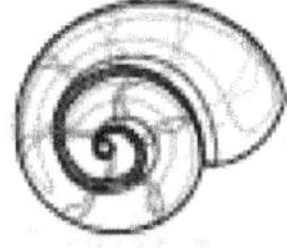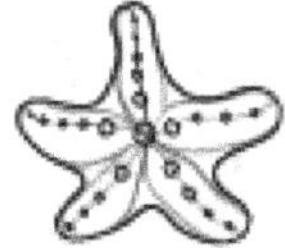

THIS DRAWING BOOK
BELONG TO

____

____

____

How to draw step by step

We've created a sketch guide by following the steps
You must repeat and transfer and with the period

with the period you will find that you learn quickly

**The first step is to draw
the head in a simple way**

**The second step is to draw and the
head of the abdomen and one of the wings**

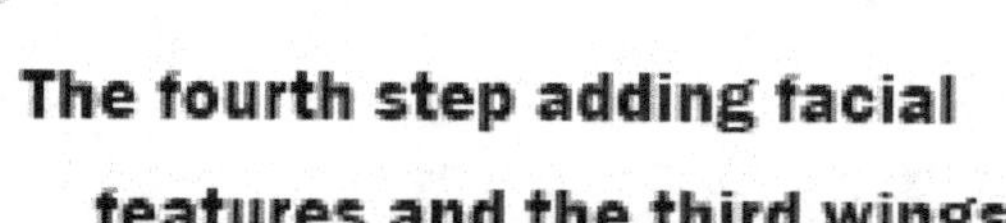

**The third step is to draw
the guilt and two wings**

**The fourth step adding facial
features and the third wings**

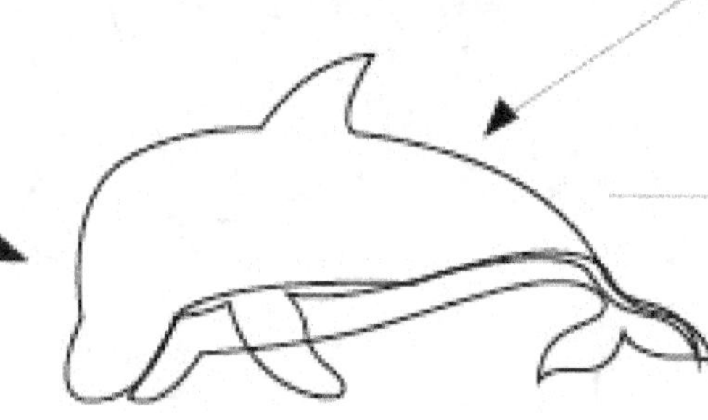

**The fifth step adding some
features of the face and abdomen**

**The sixth step is to
add the final touches**

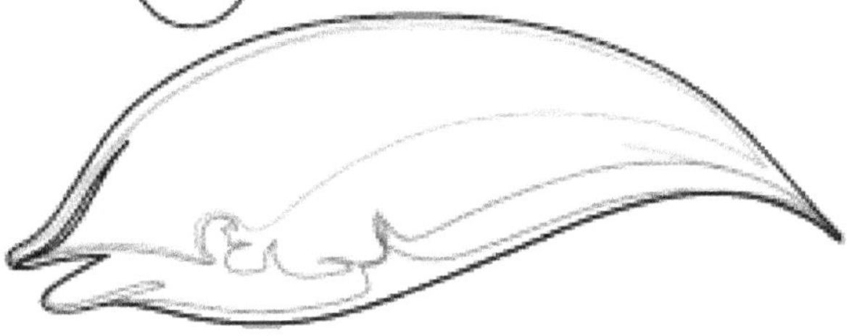

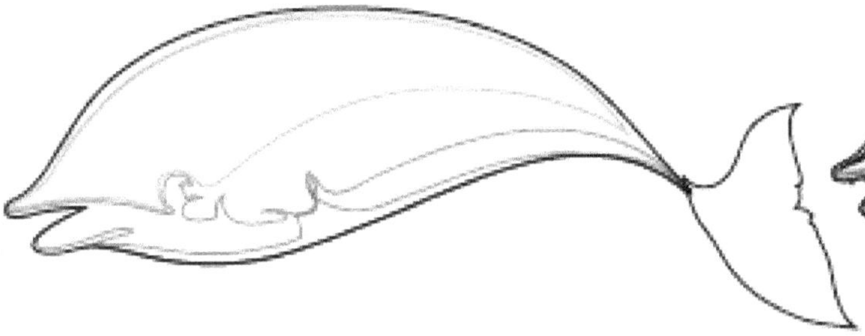

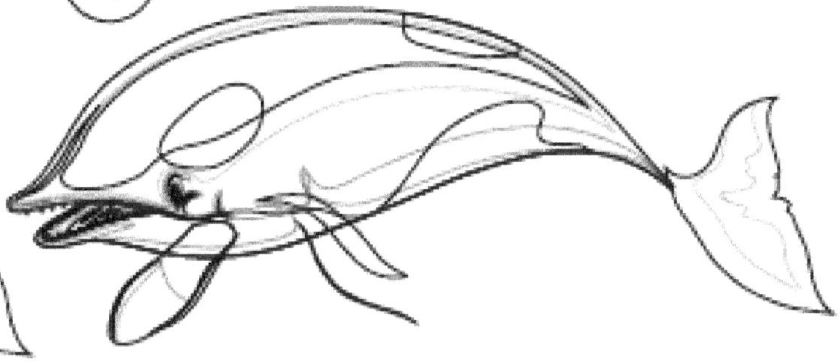

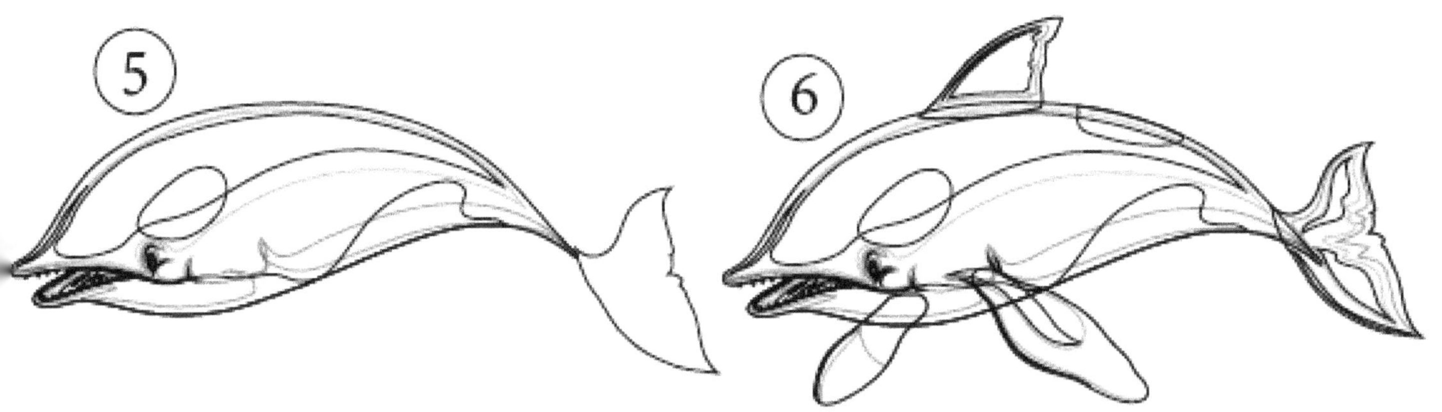

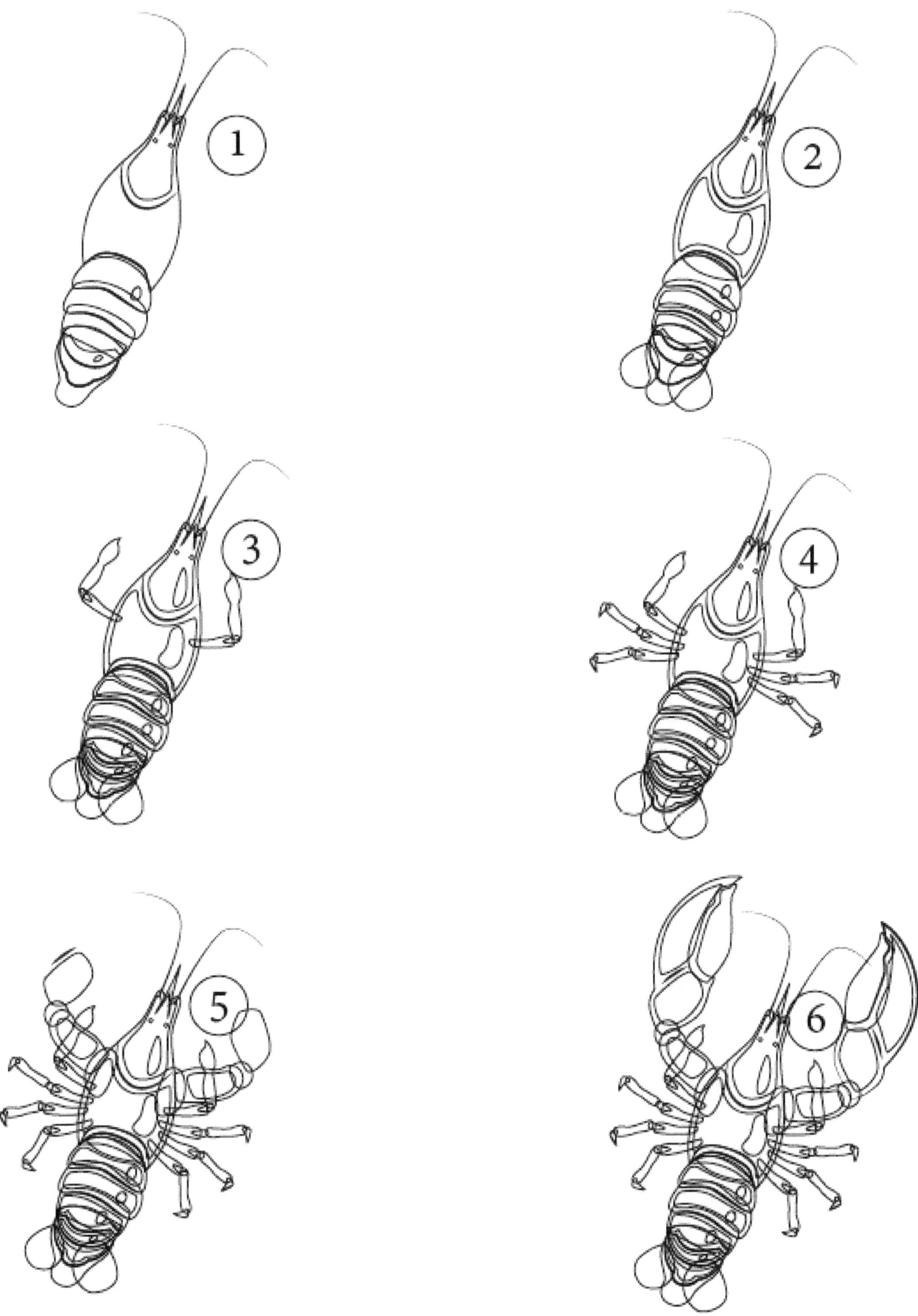

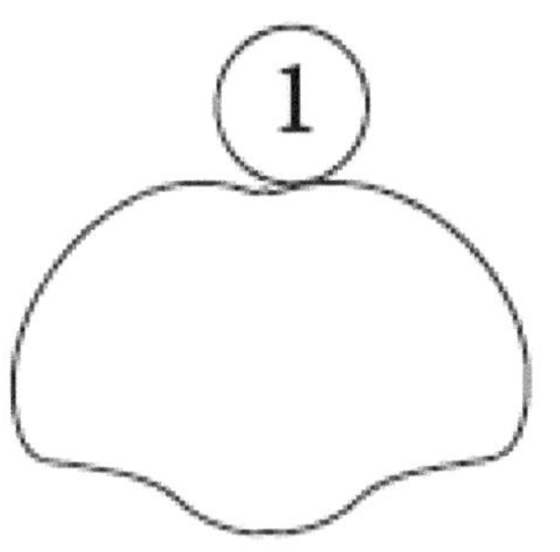

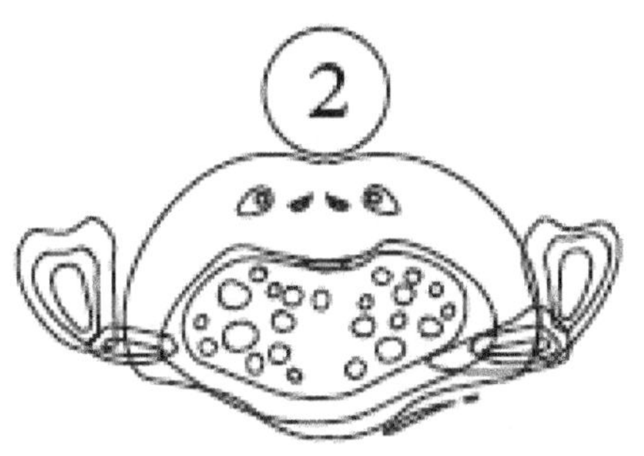

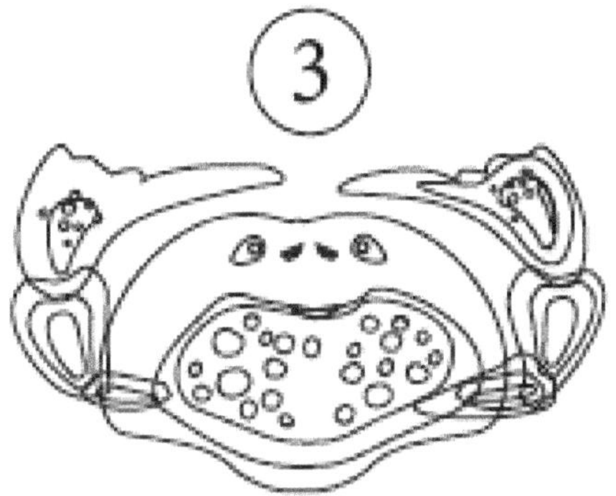

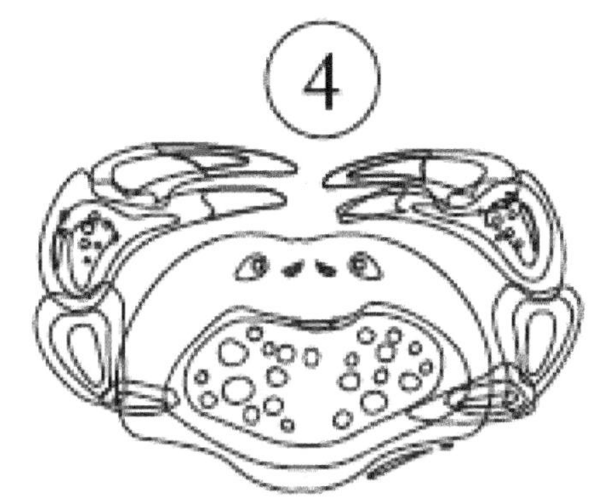

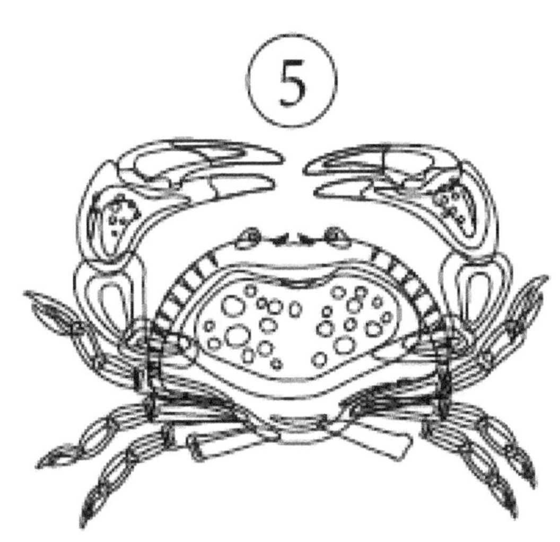

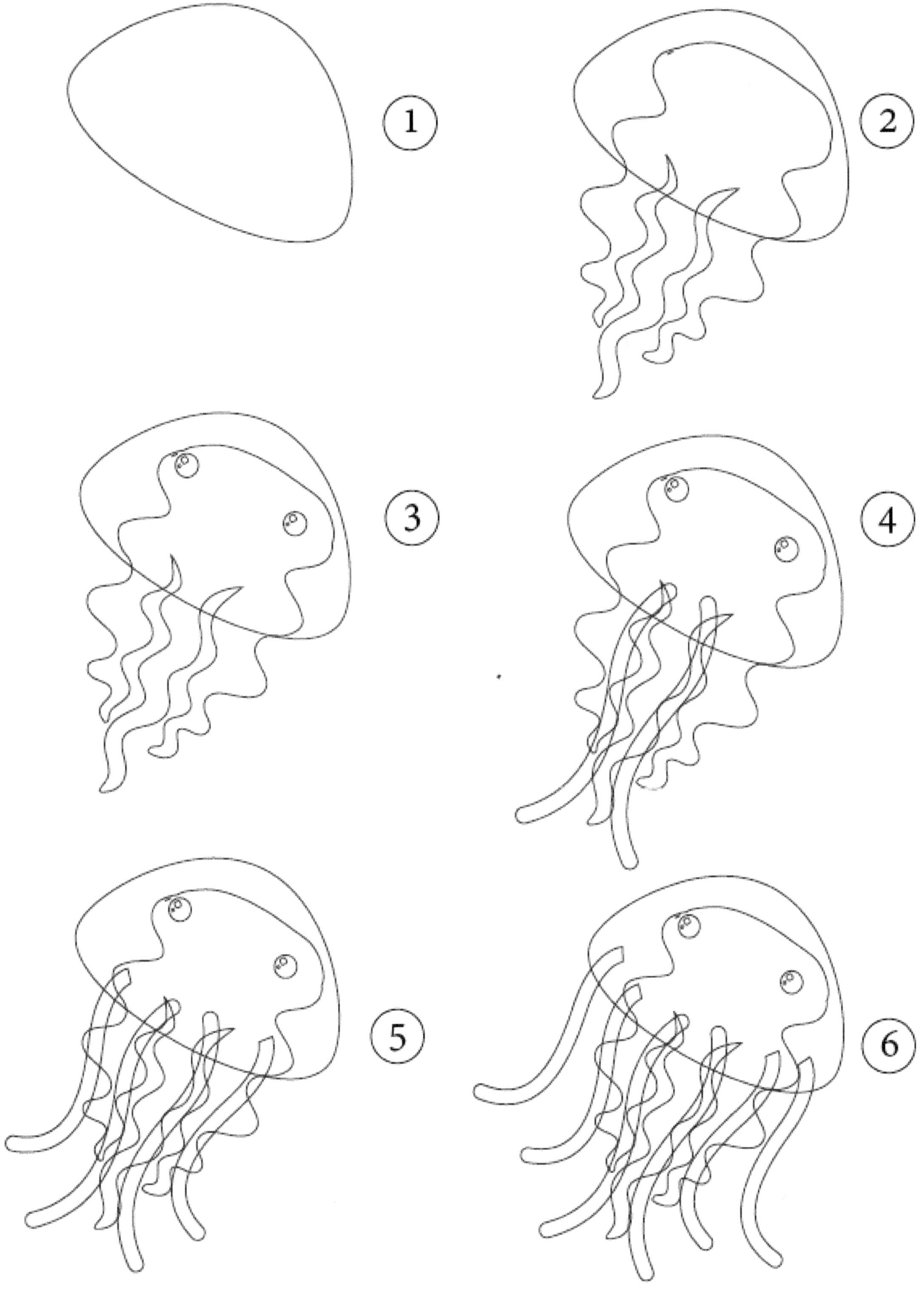

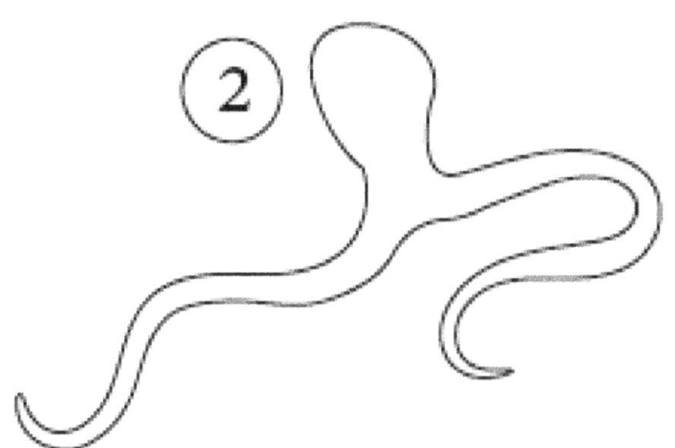

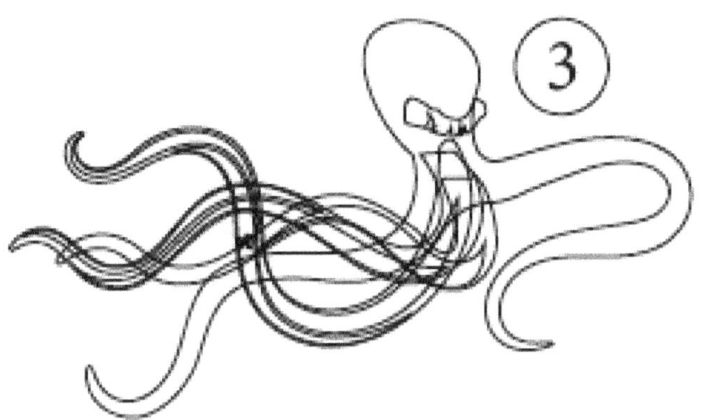

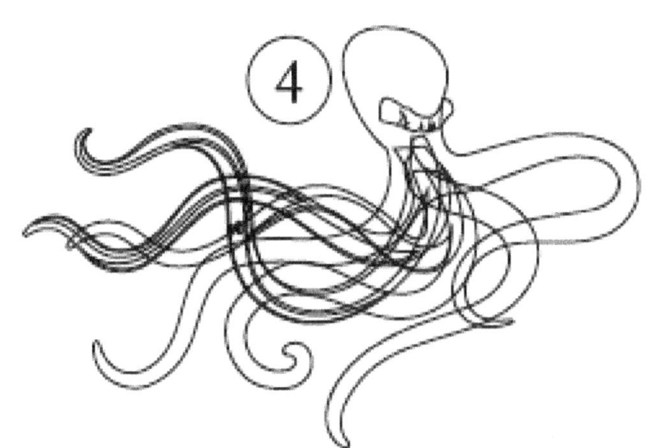

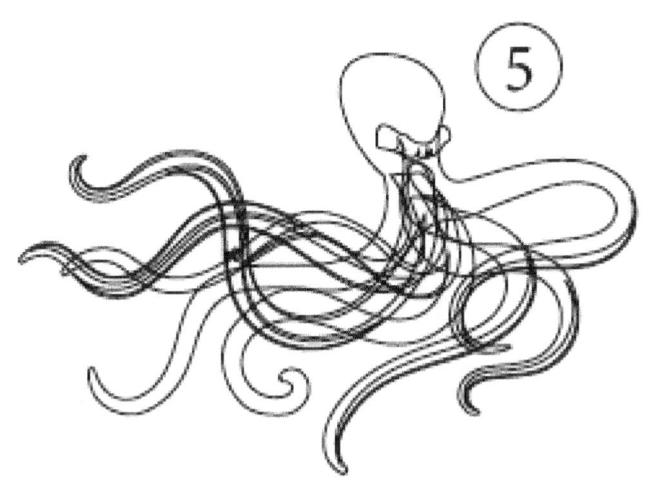

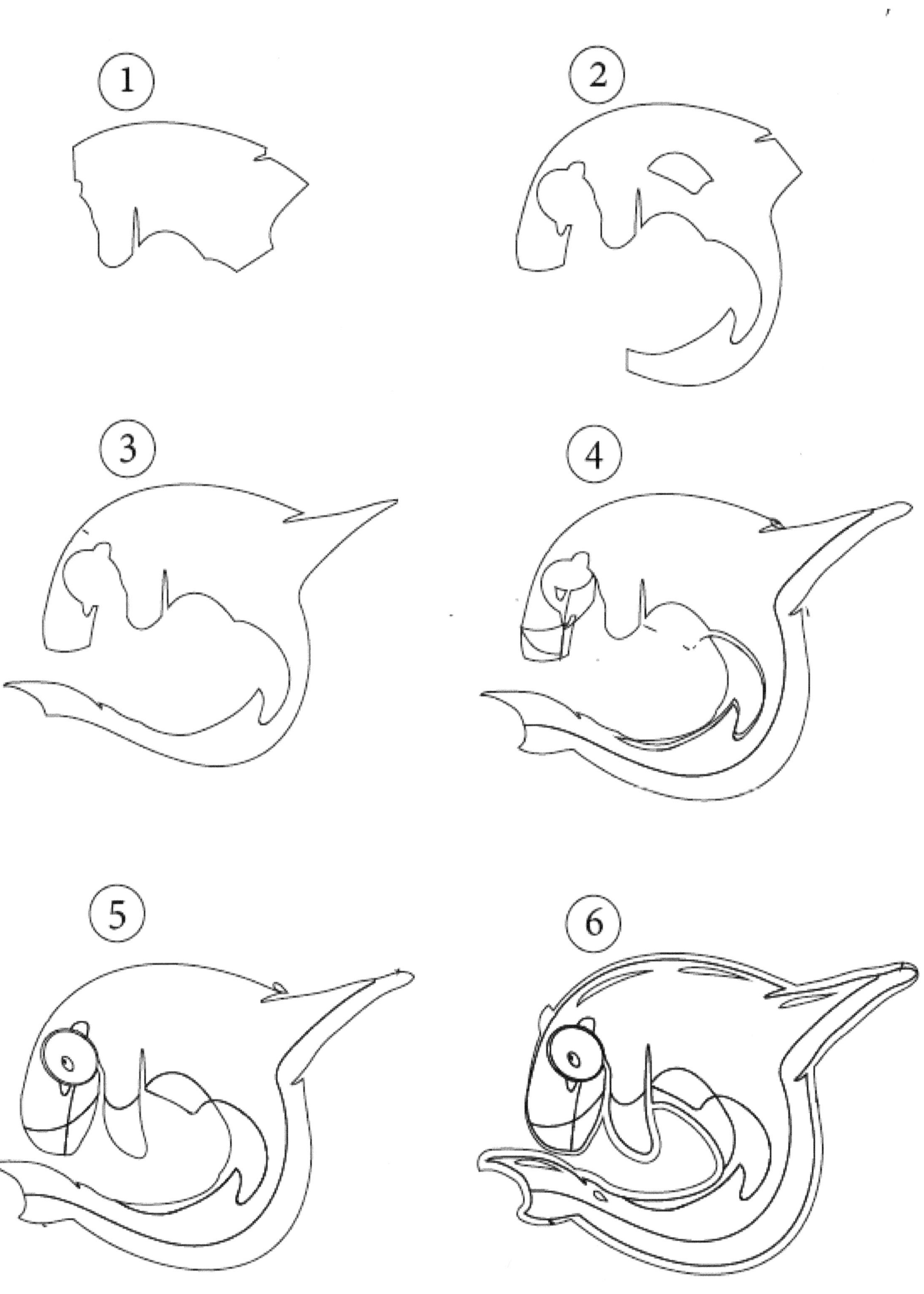

1
2
3
4
5
6

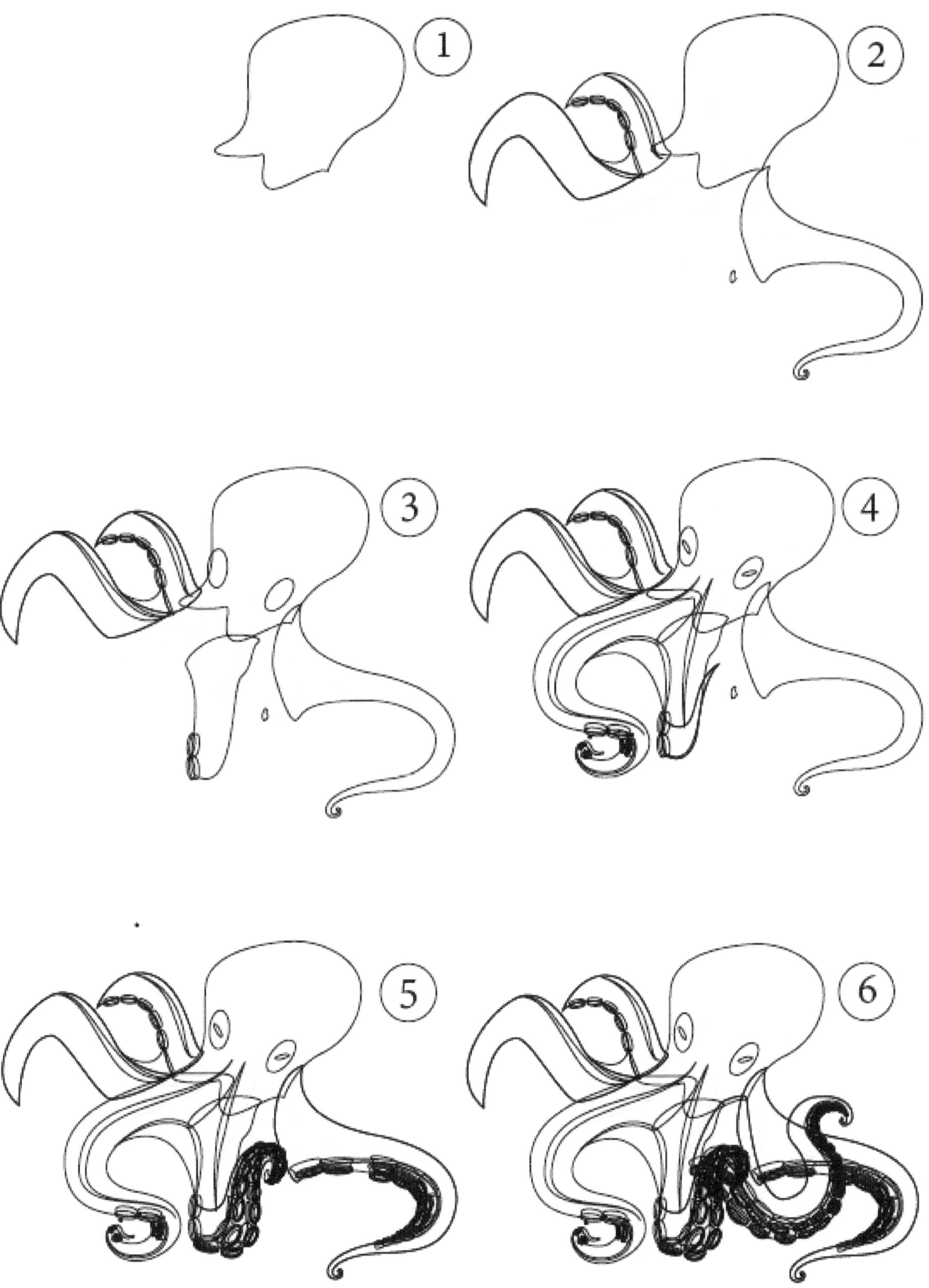

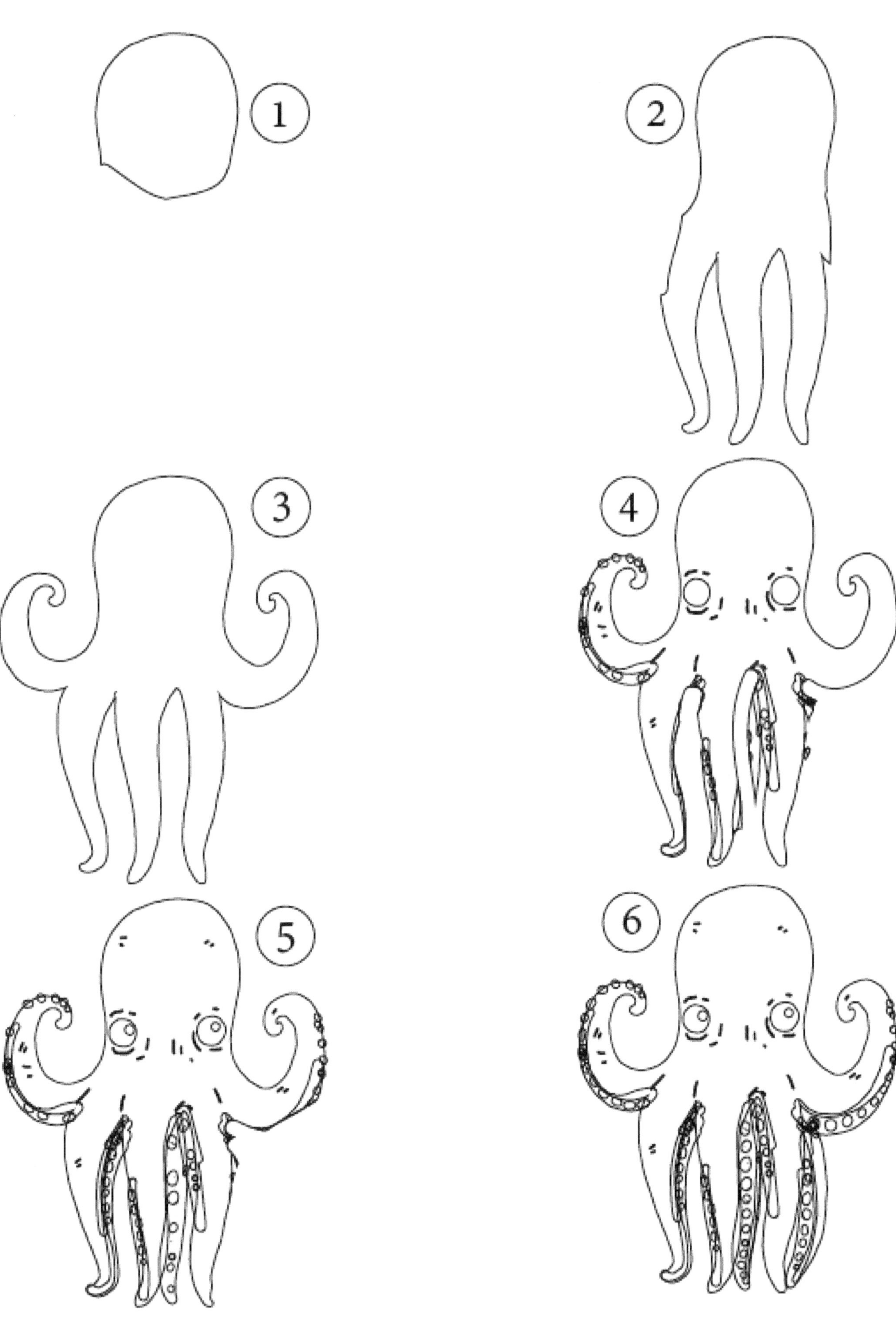

1
2
3
4
5
6

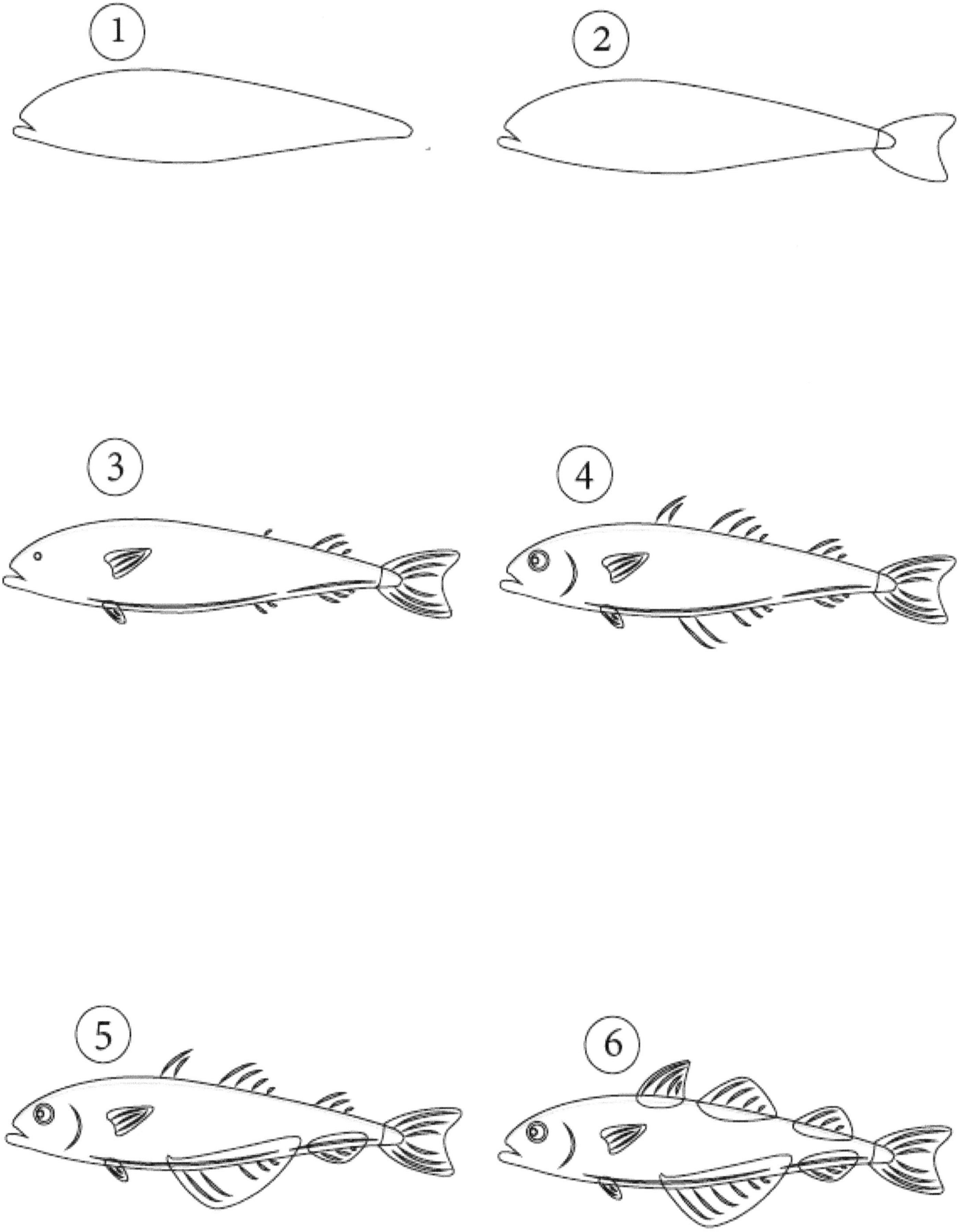

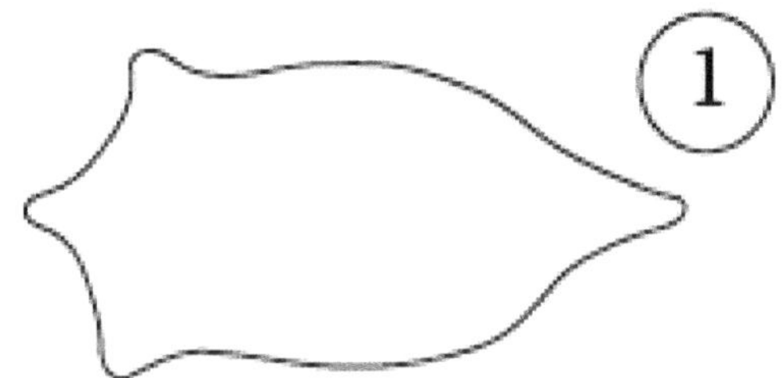

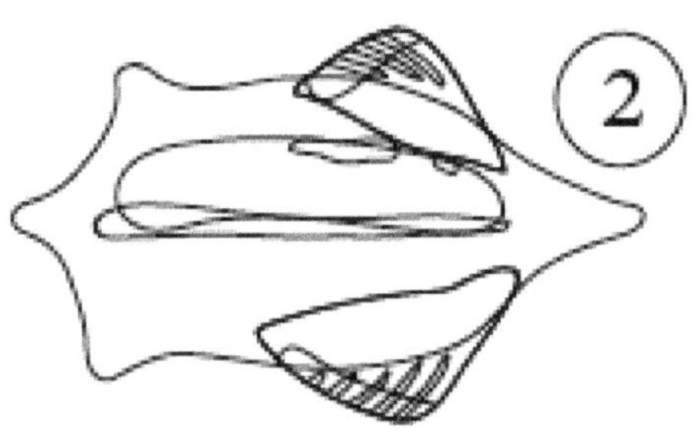

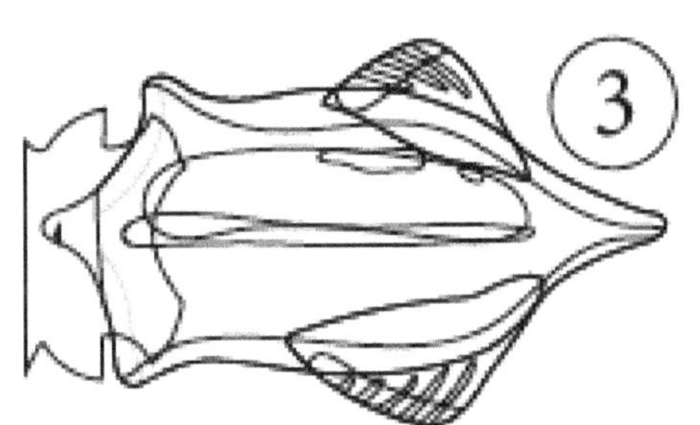

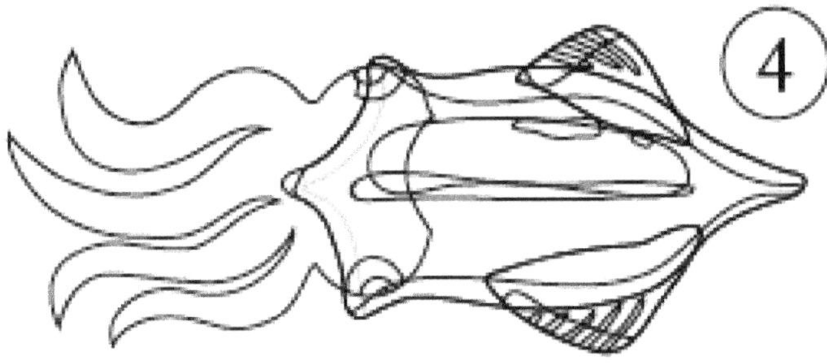

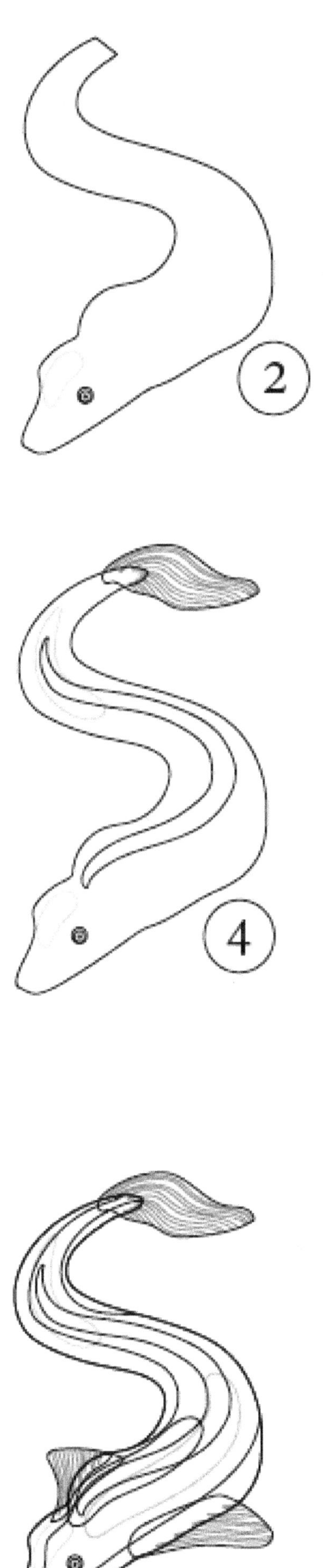
1
2
3 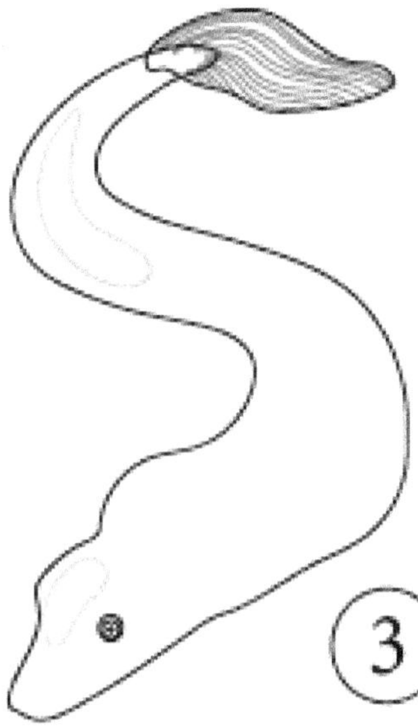
4
5 
6

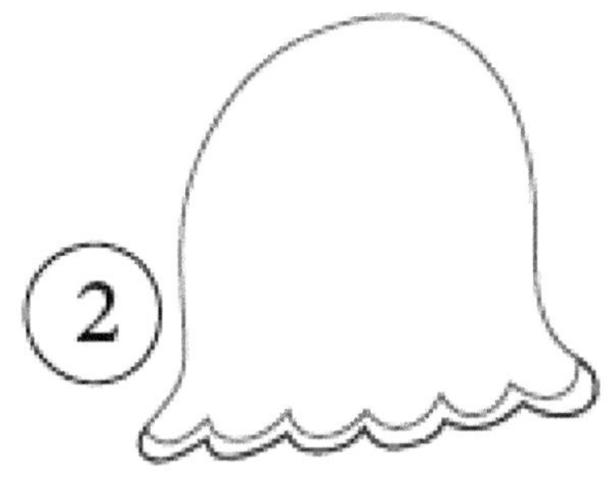

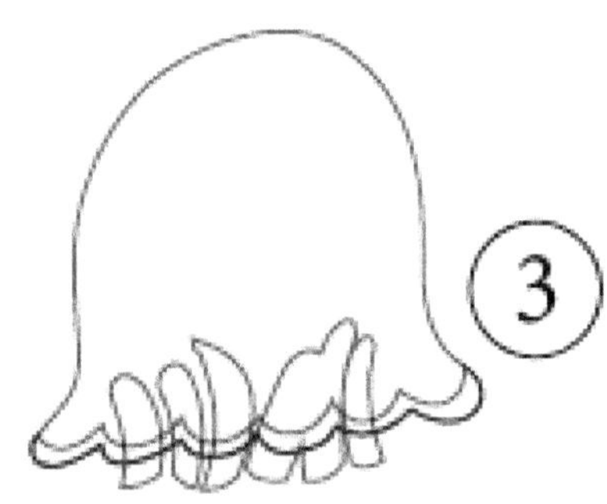

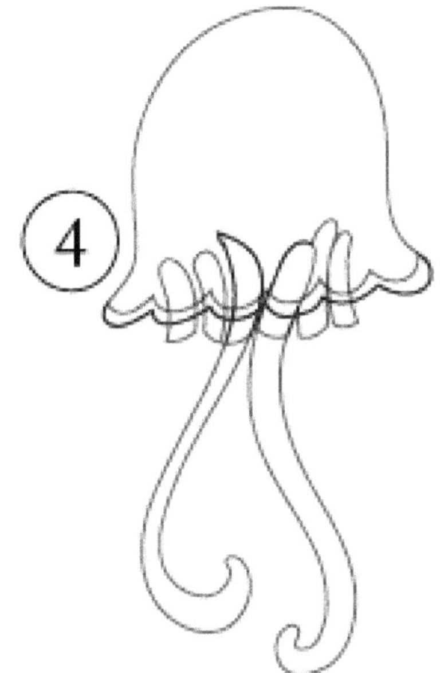

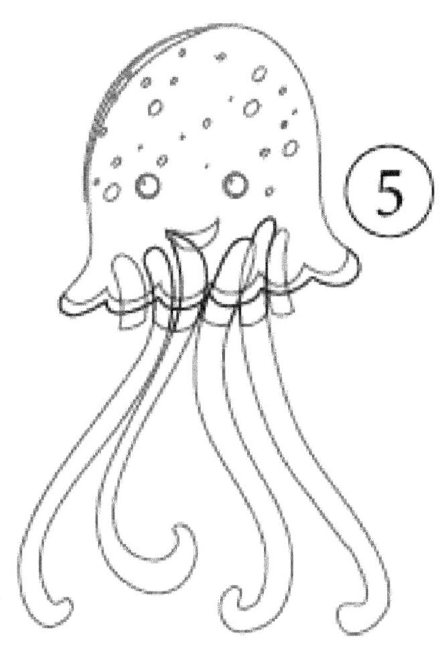

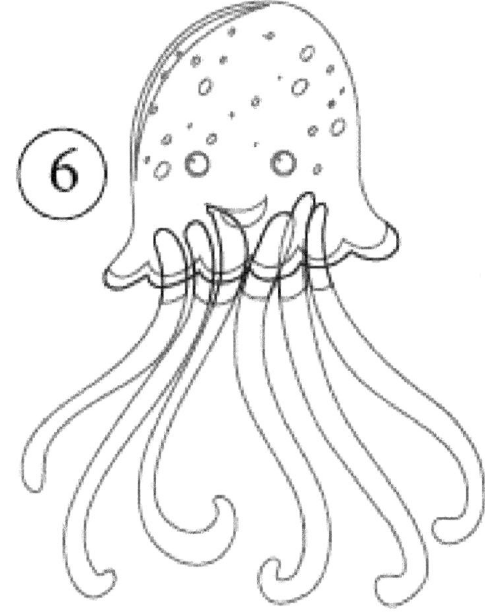

1
2
3
4
5
6

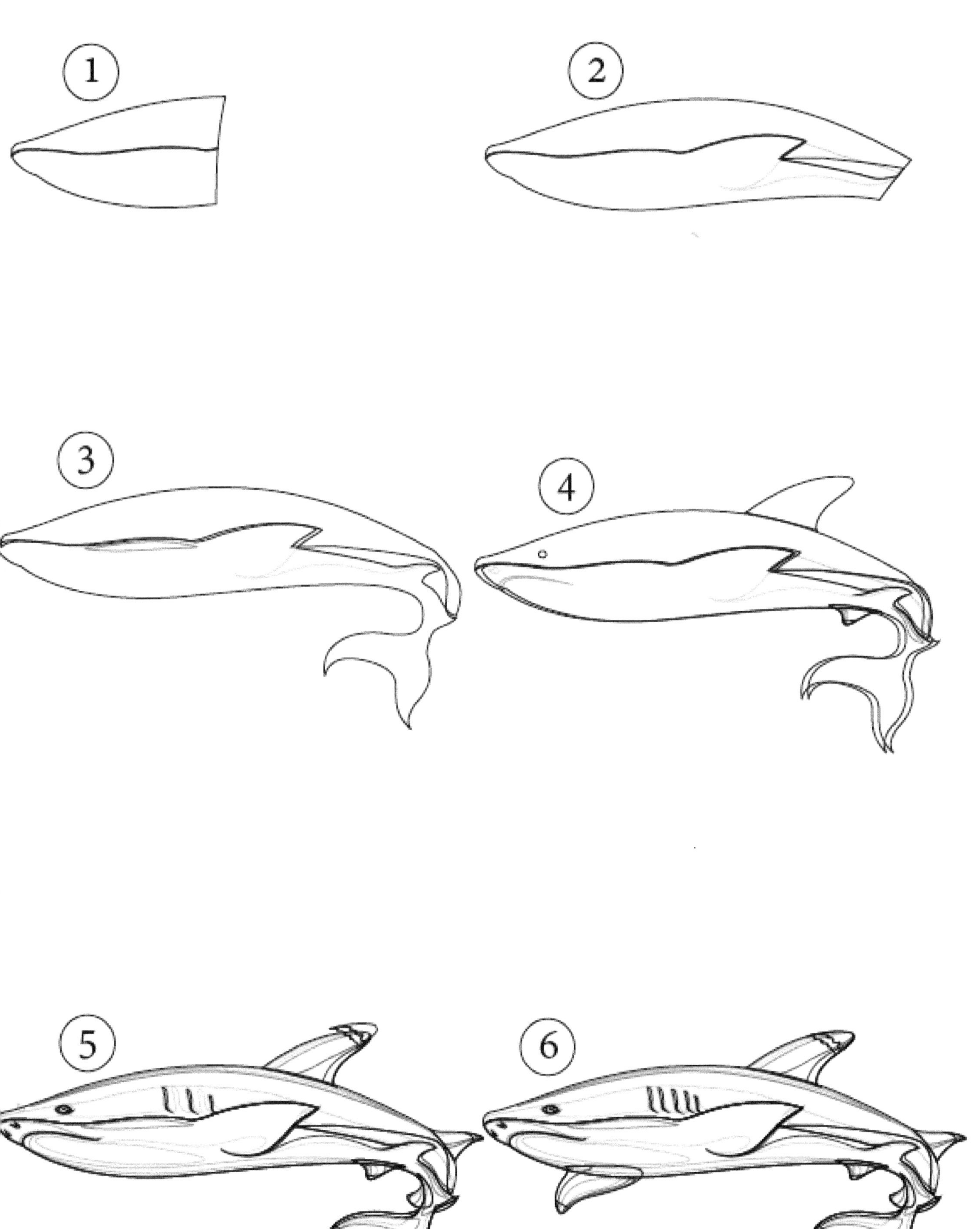

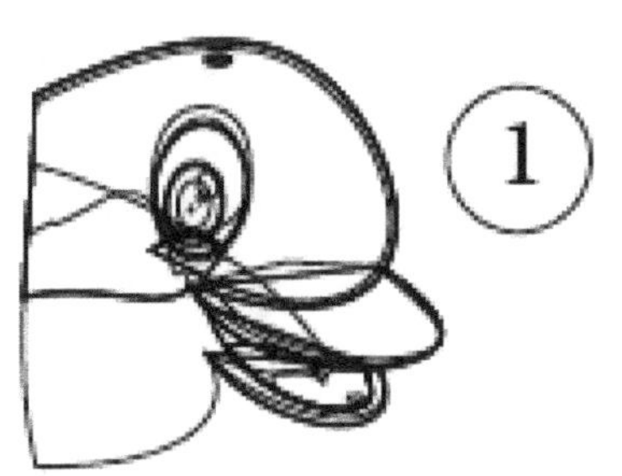

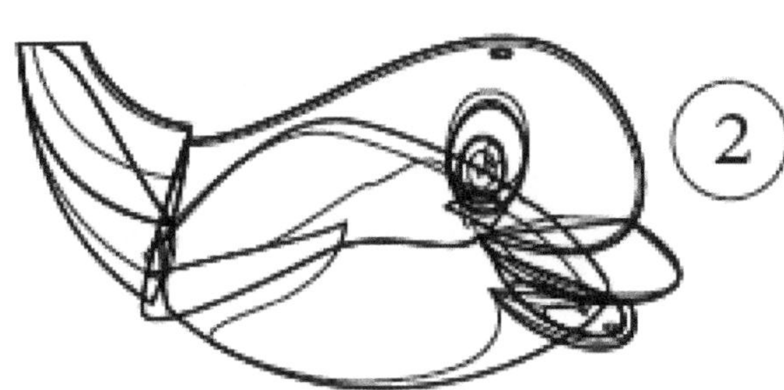

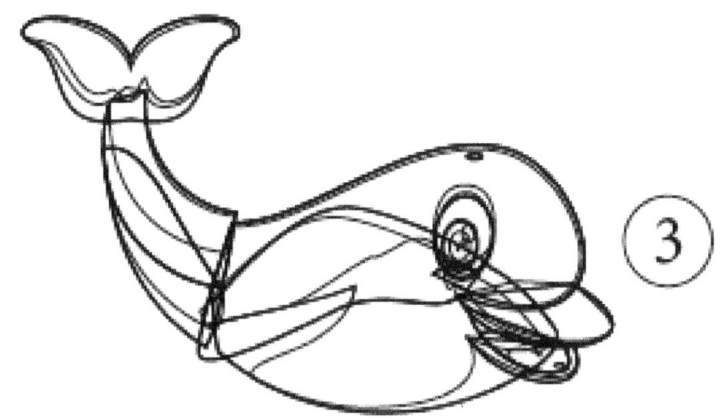

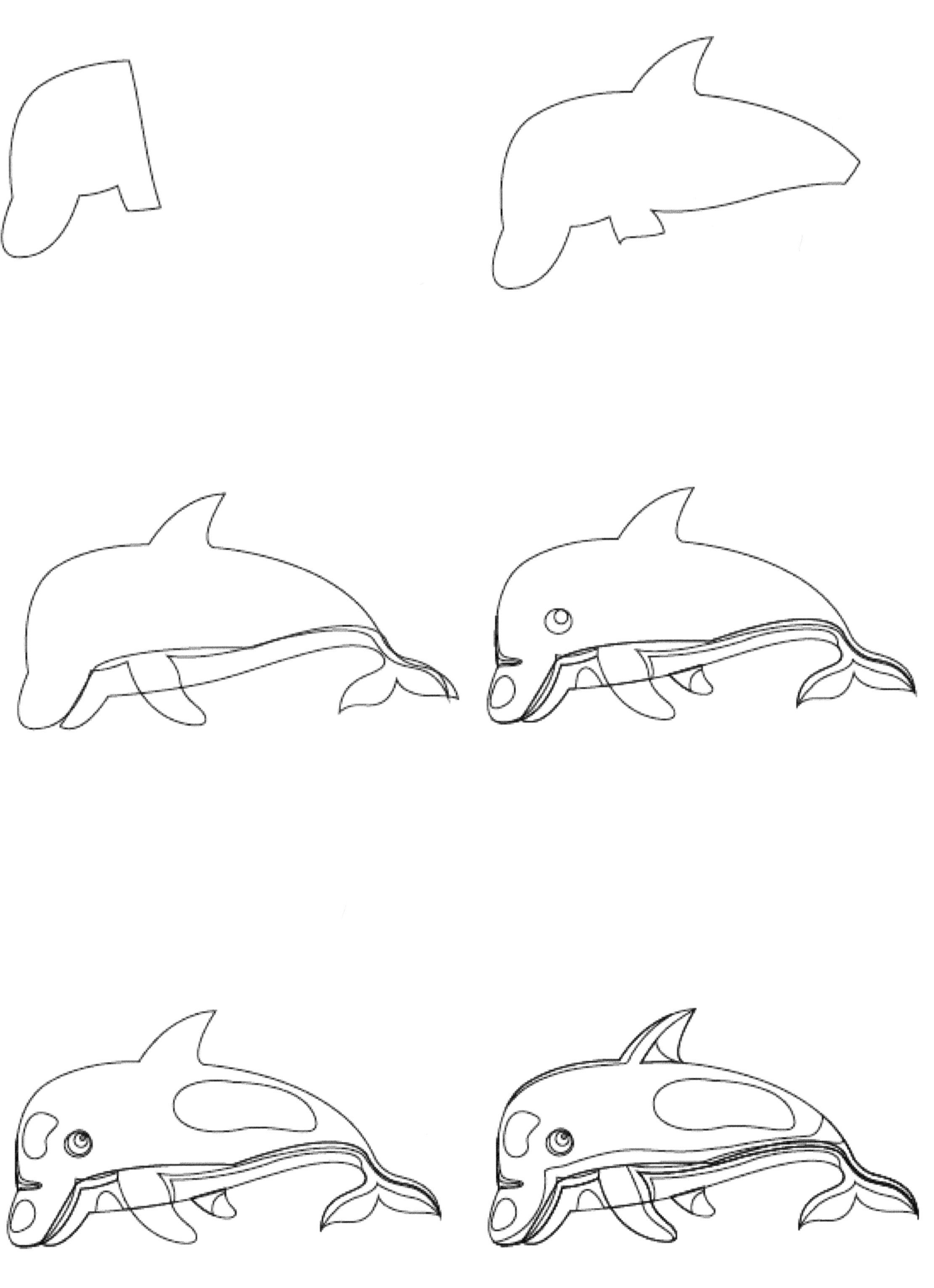

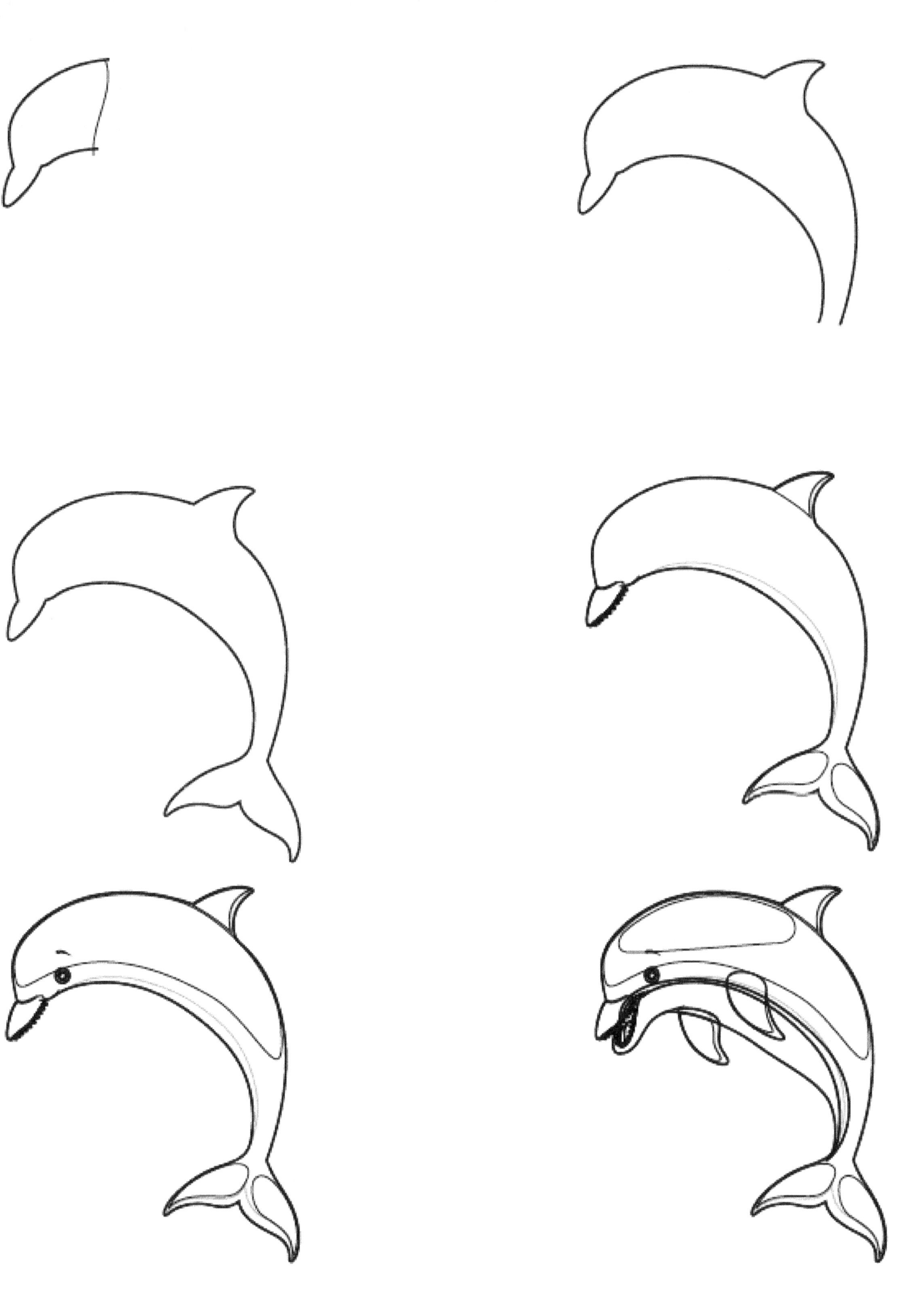

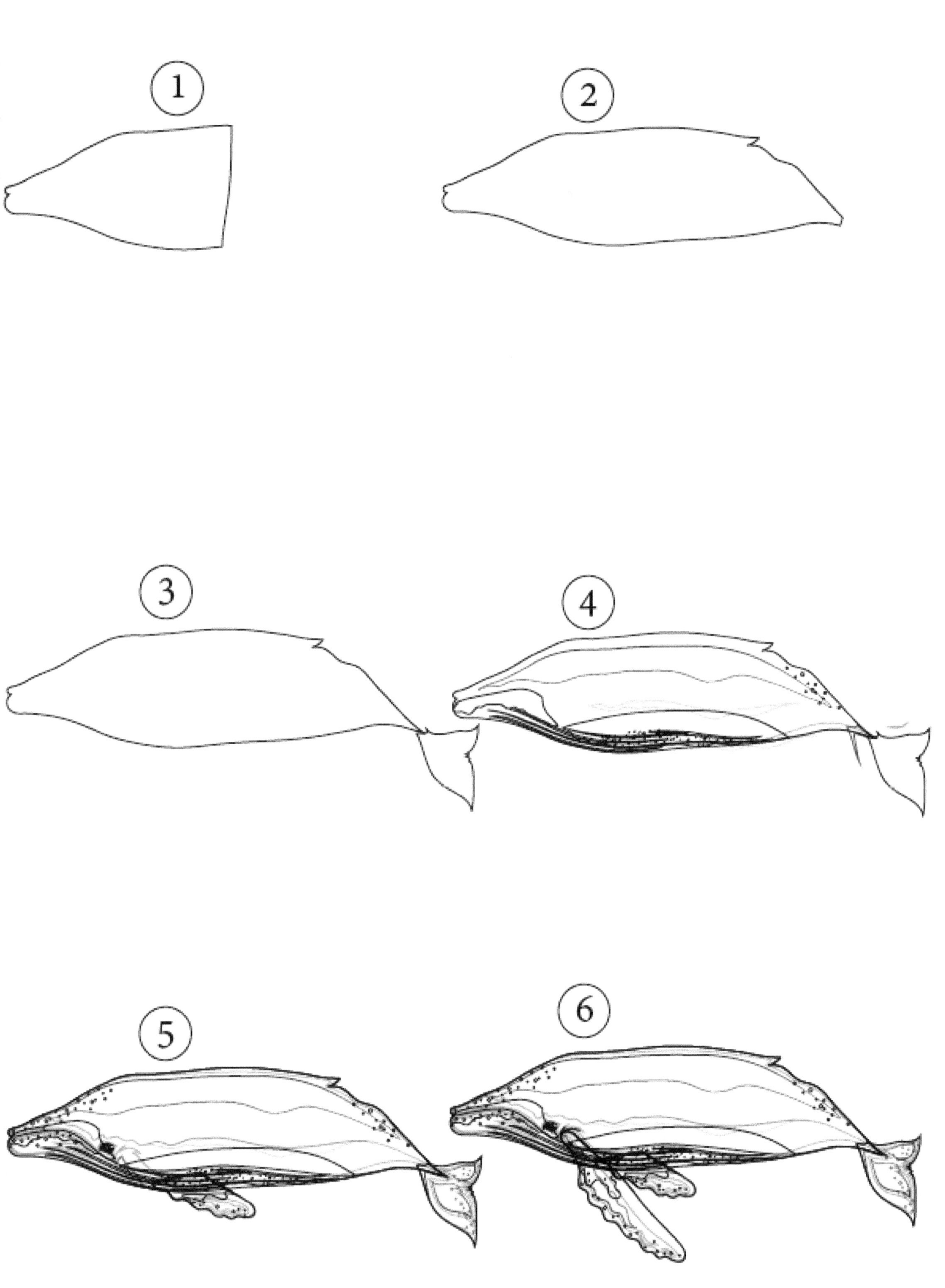

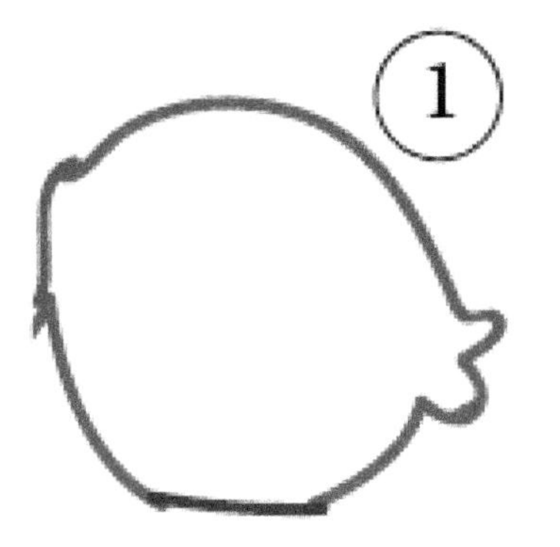

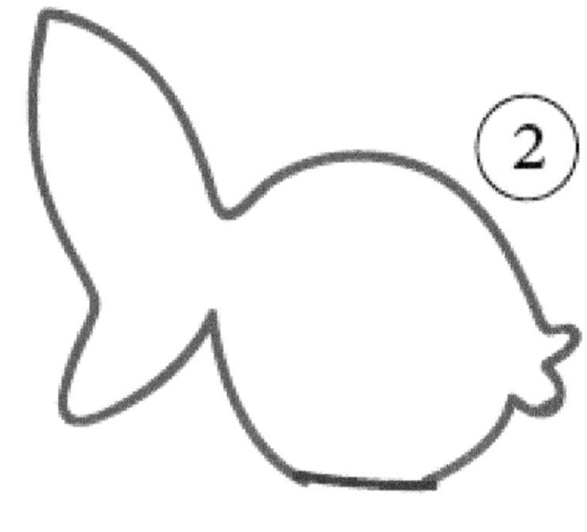

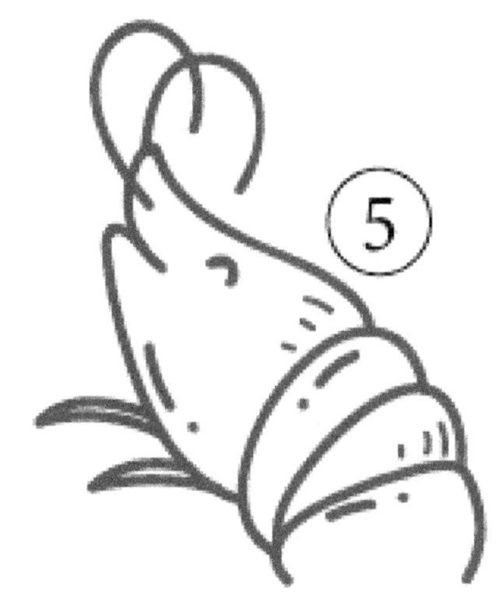

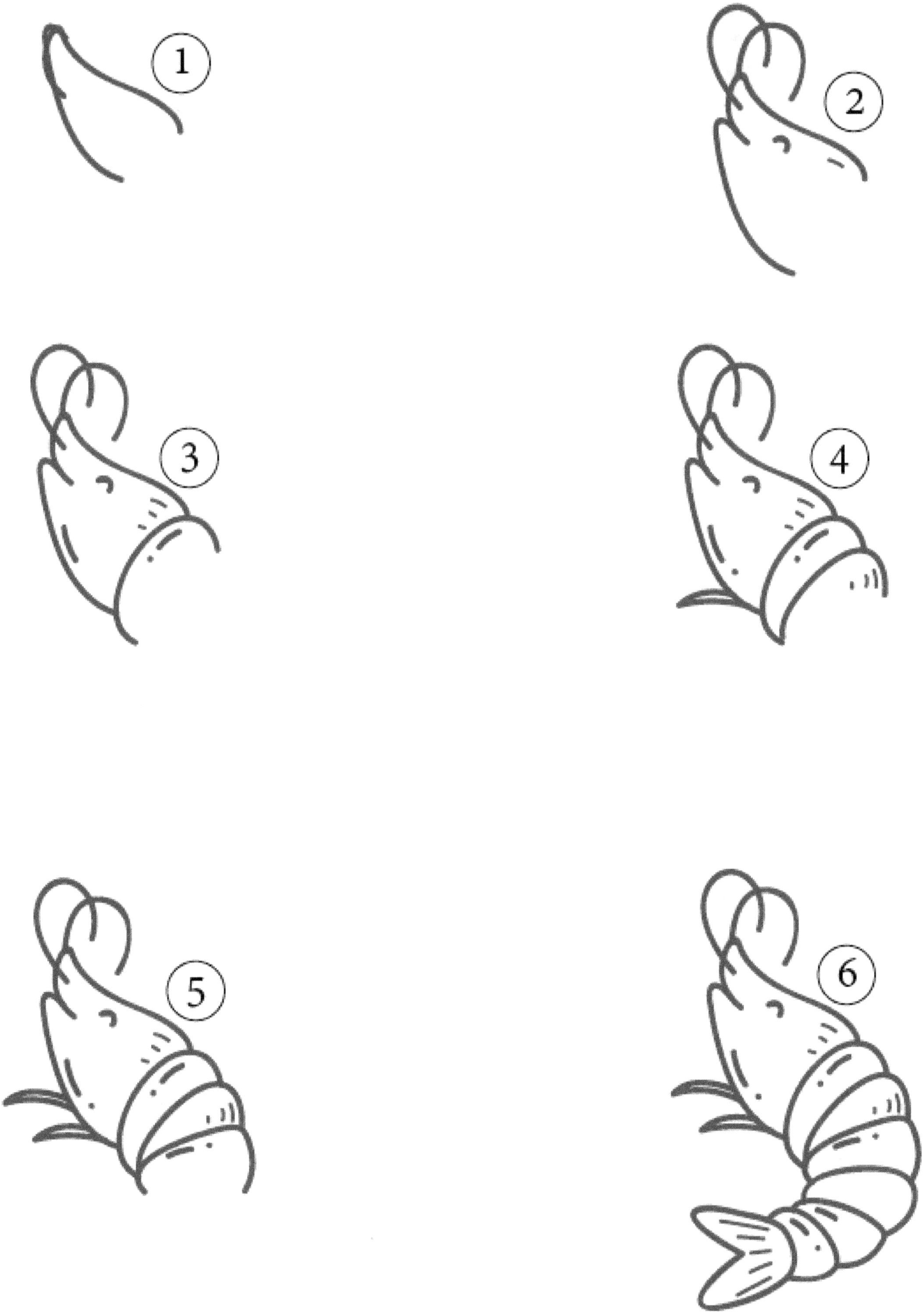

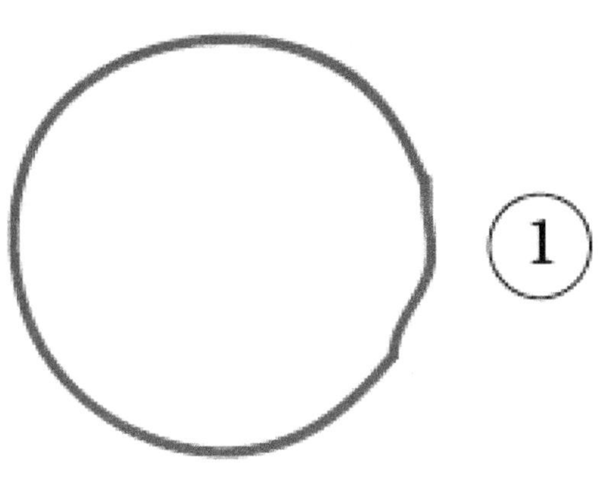

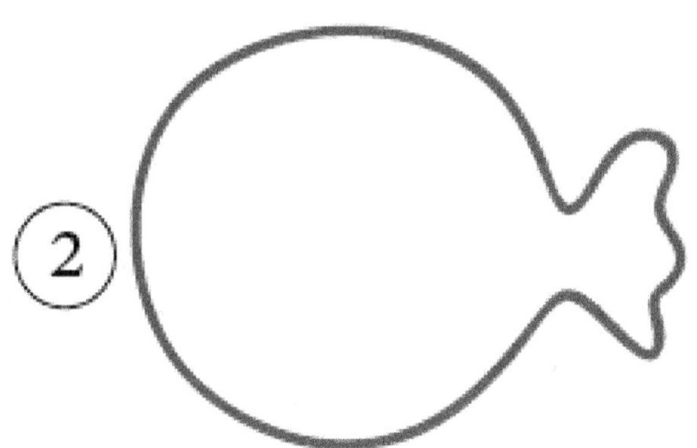

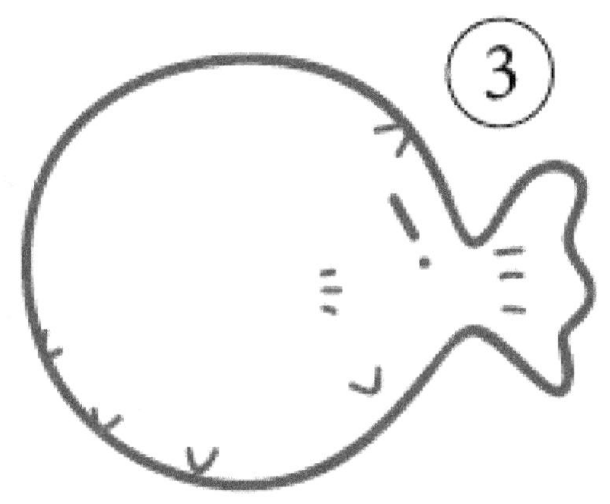

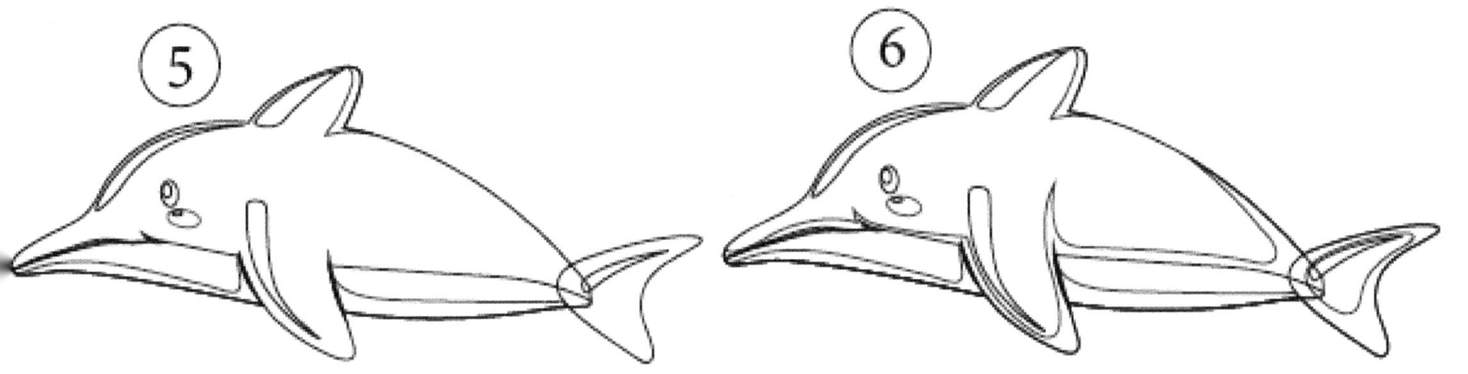

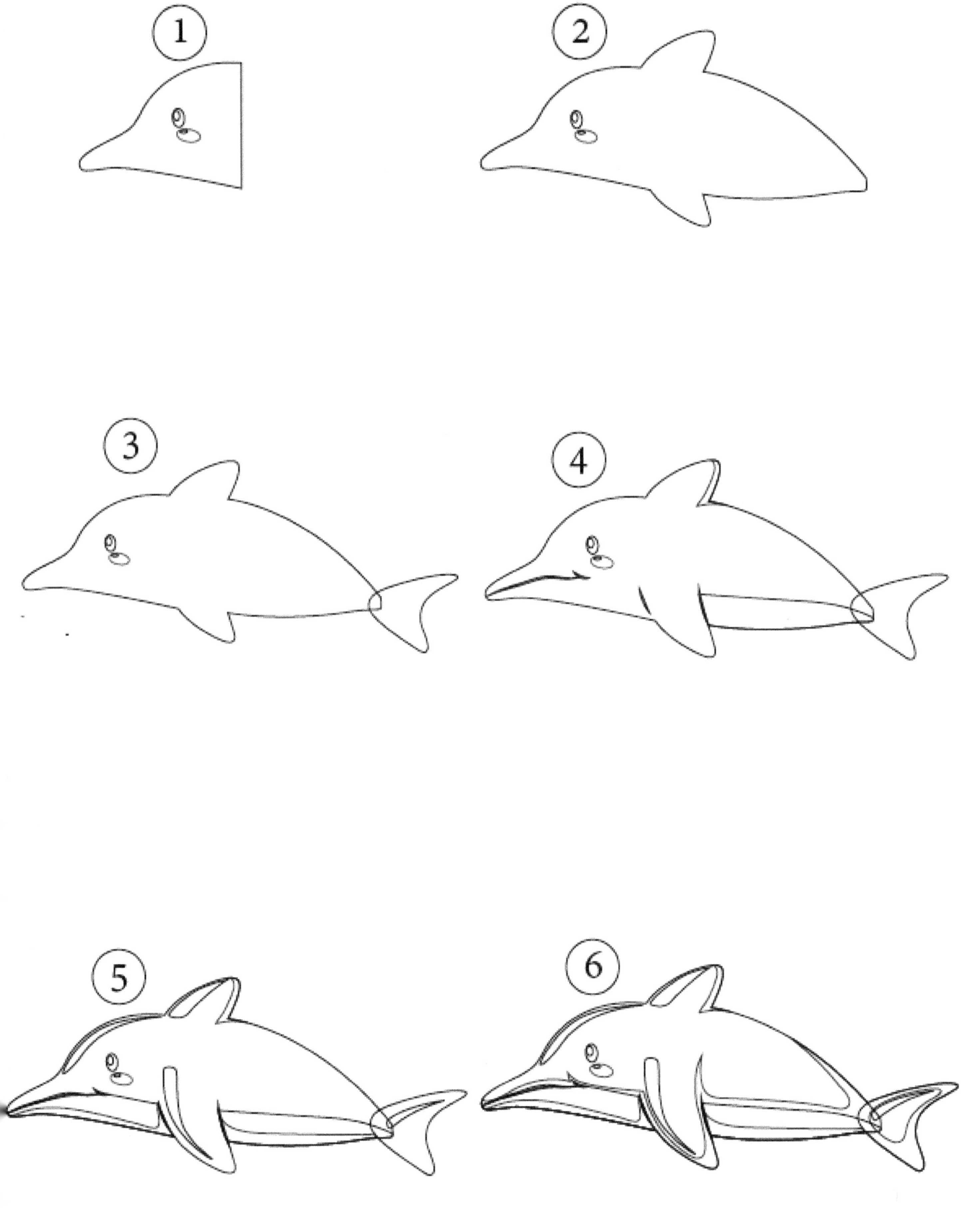

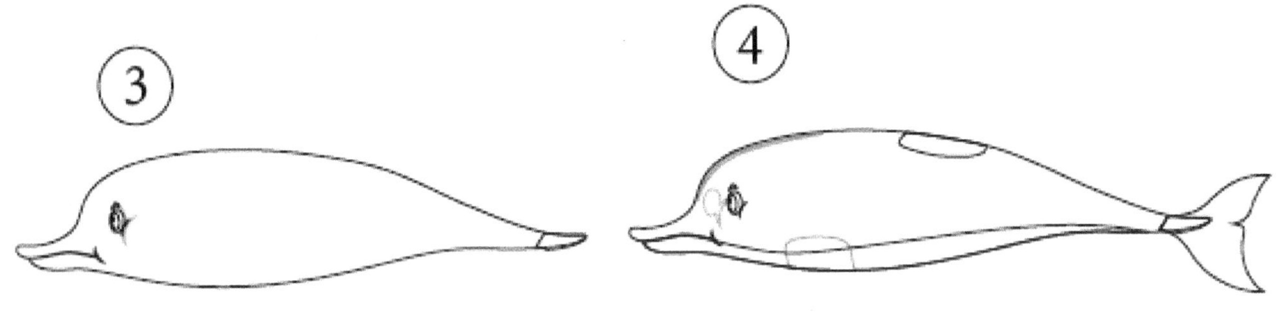

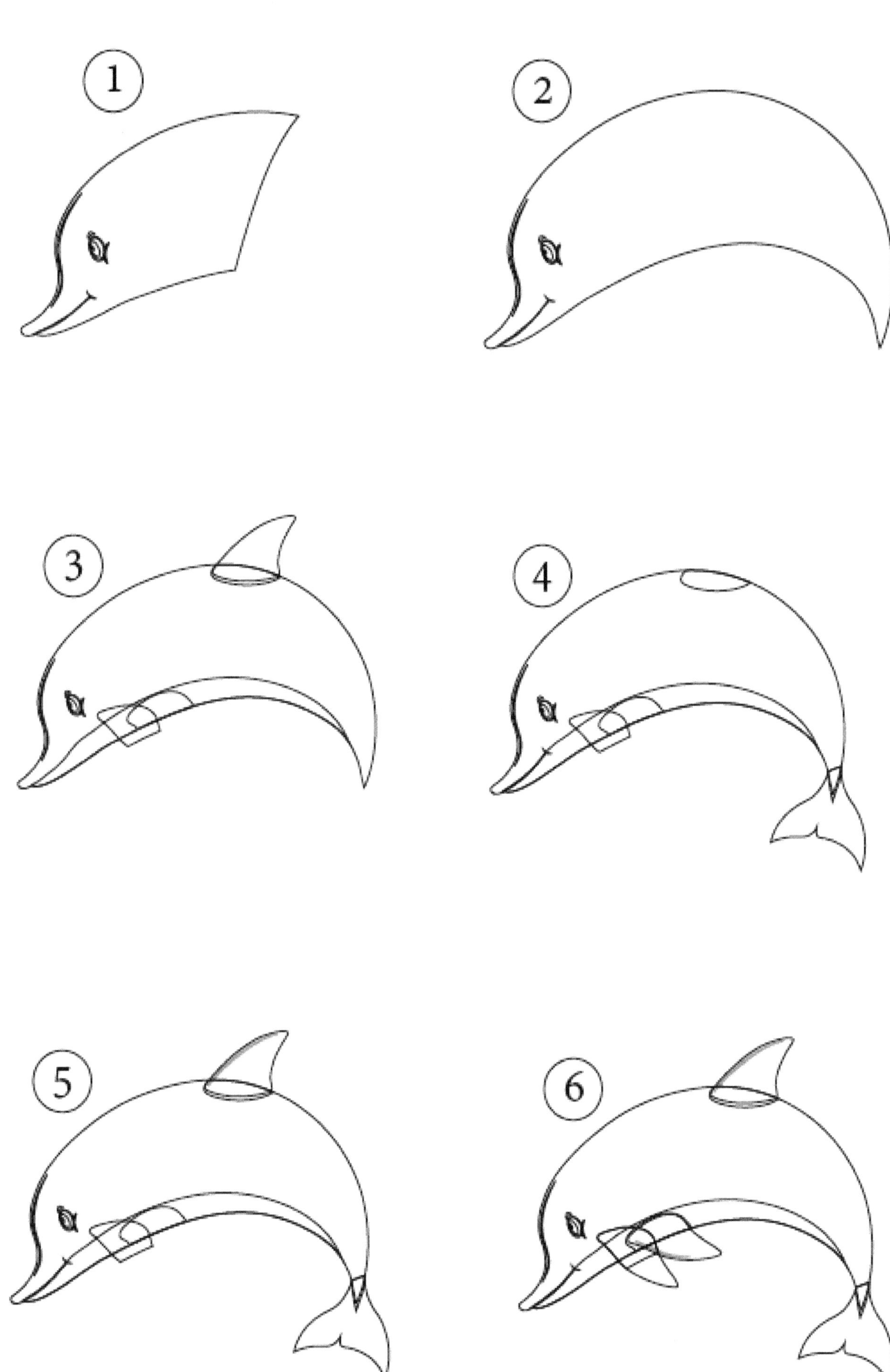

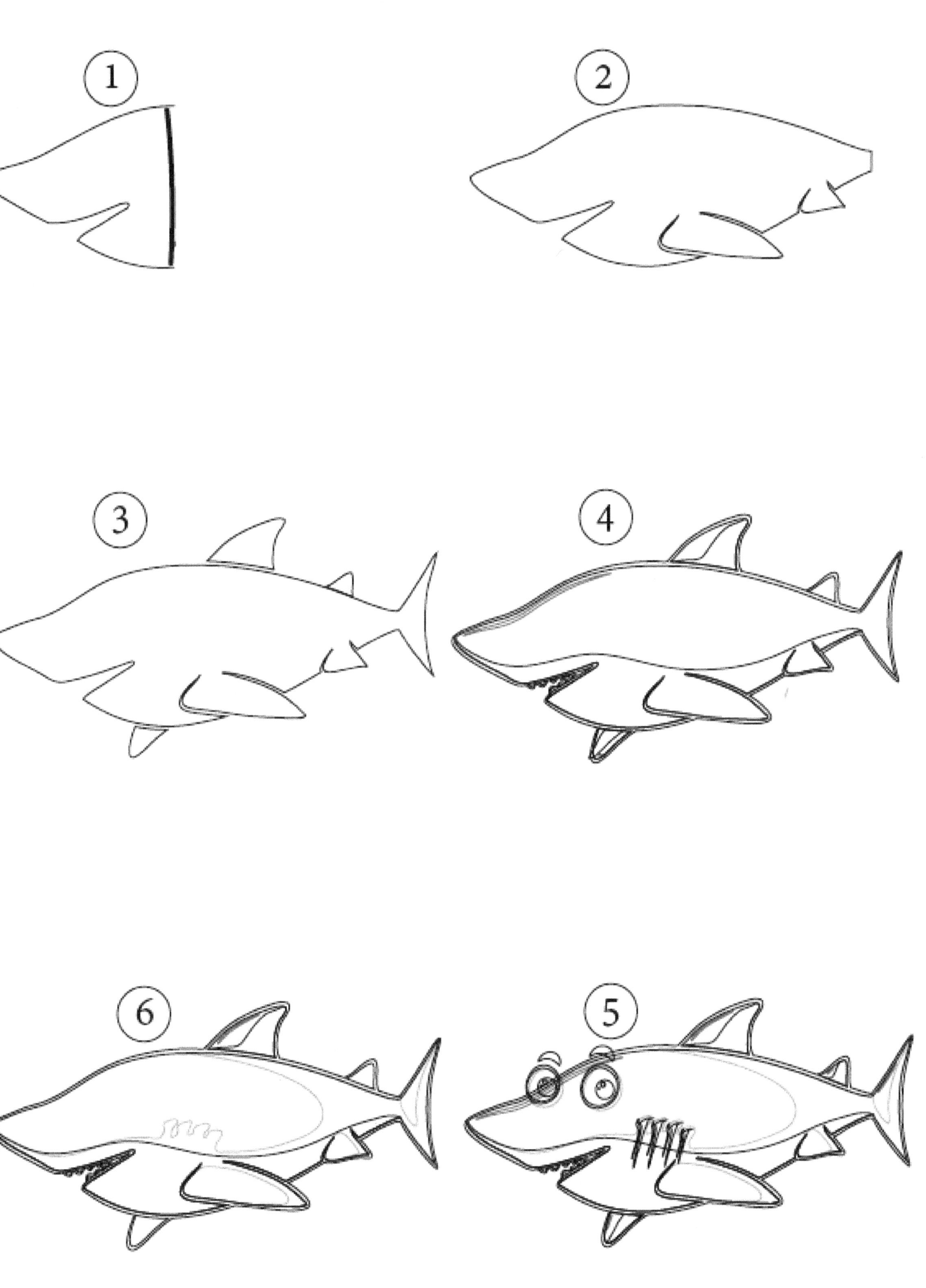

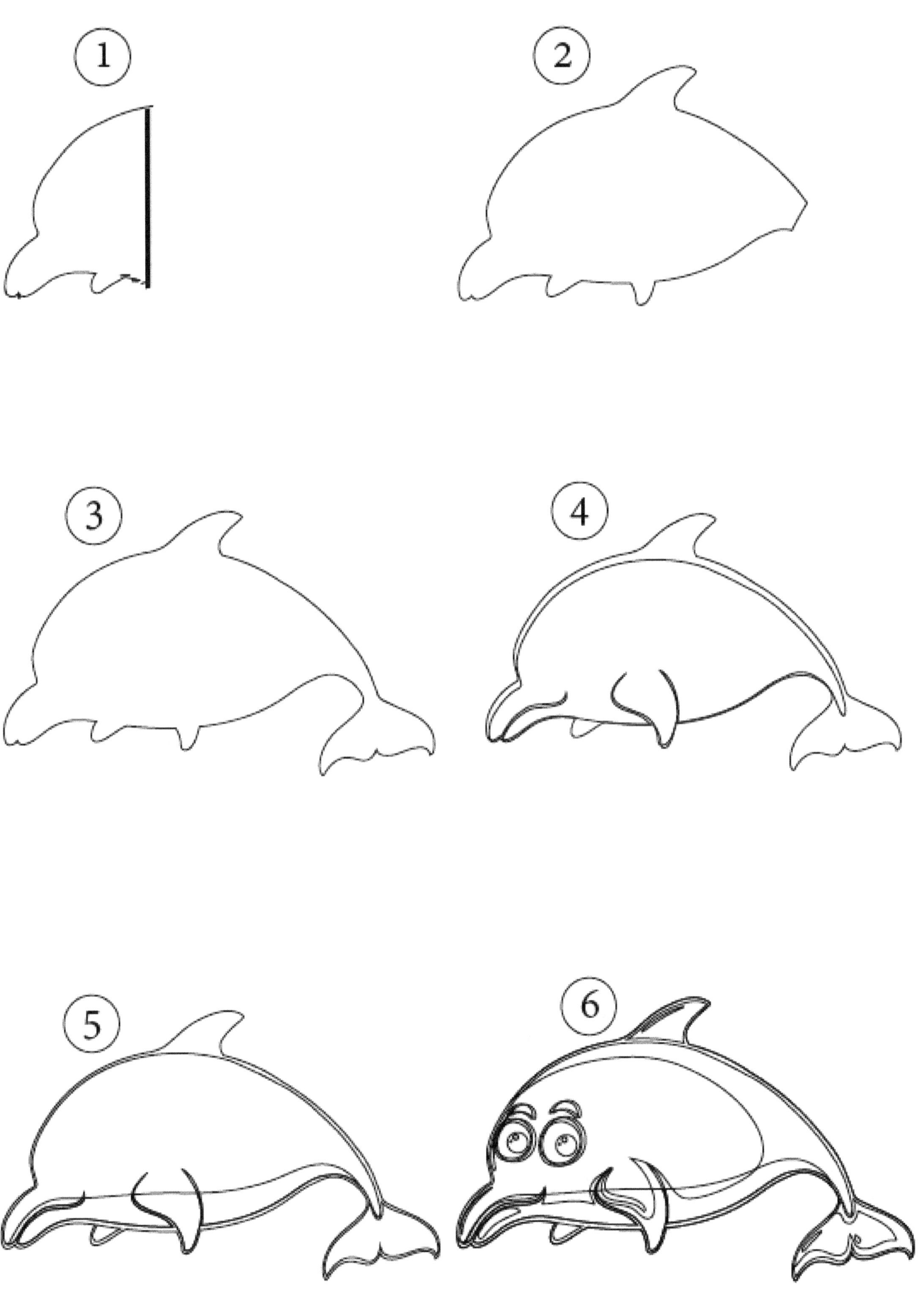

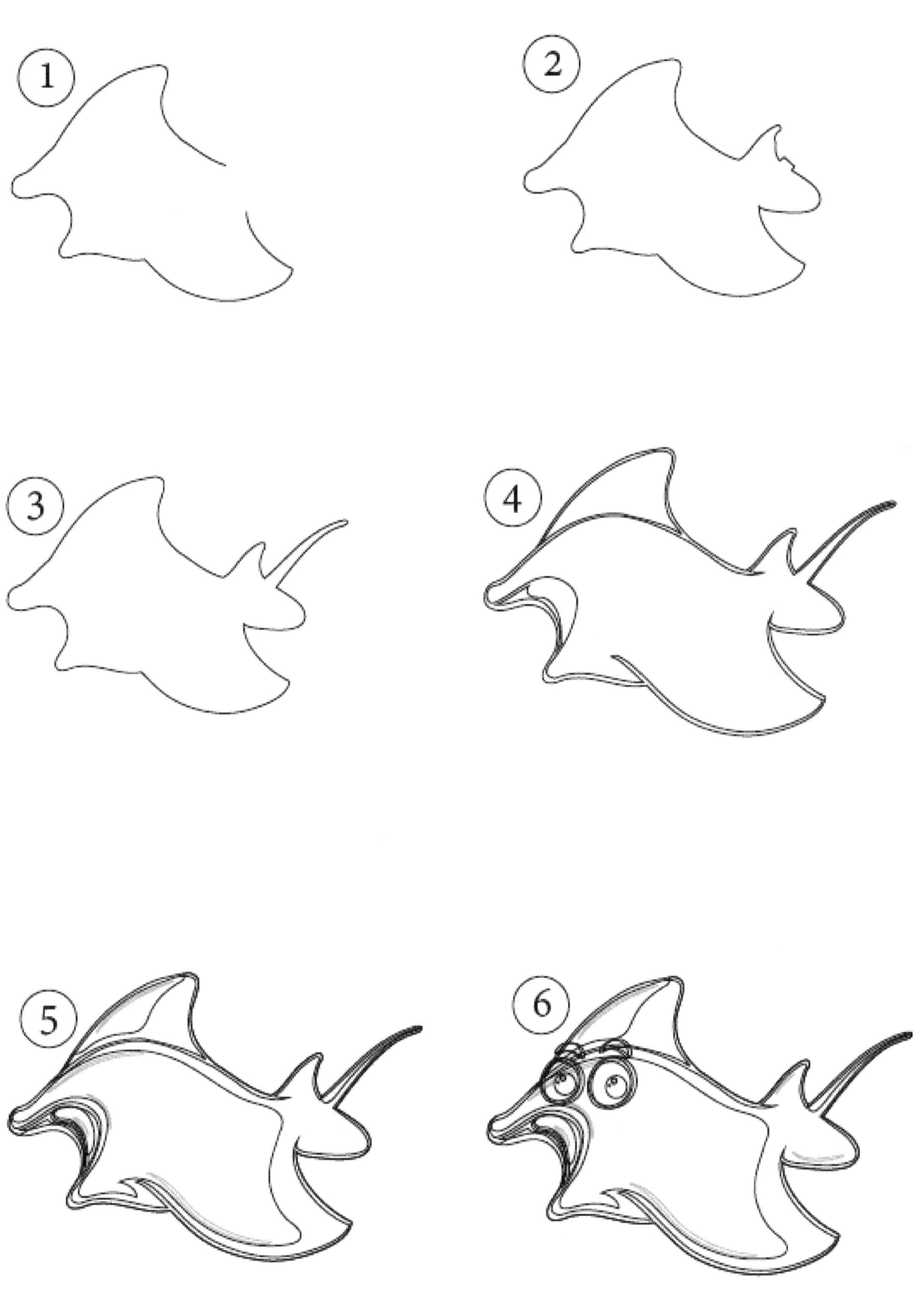

1
2
3
4
5
6

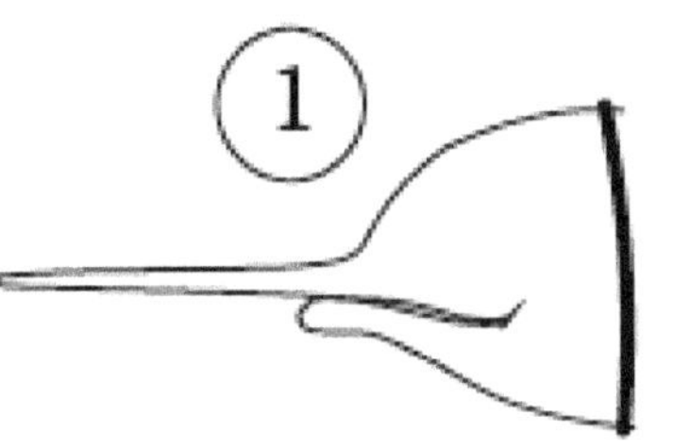

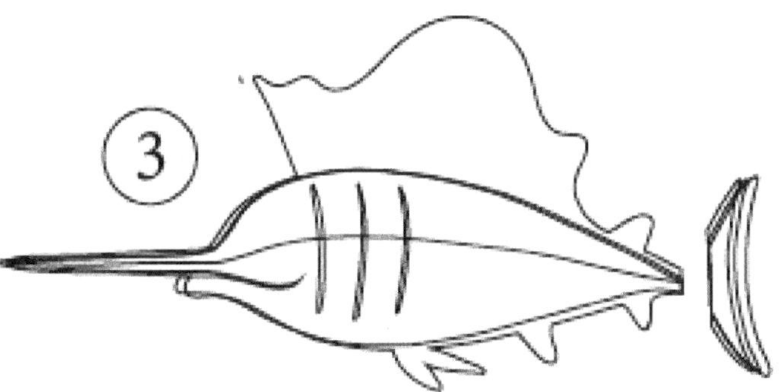

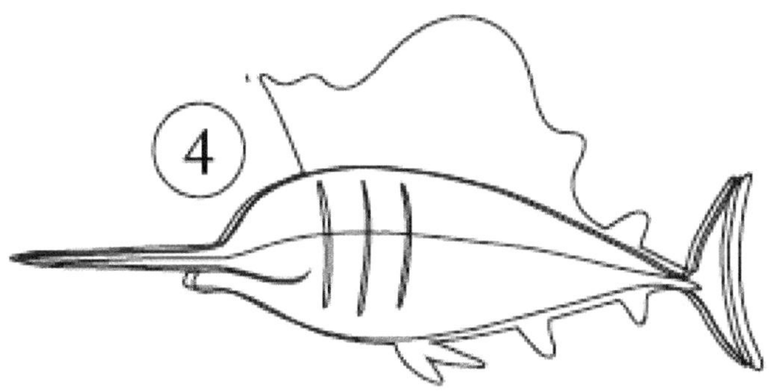

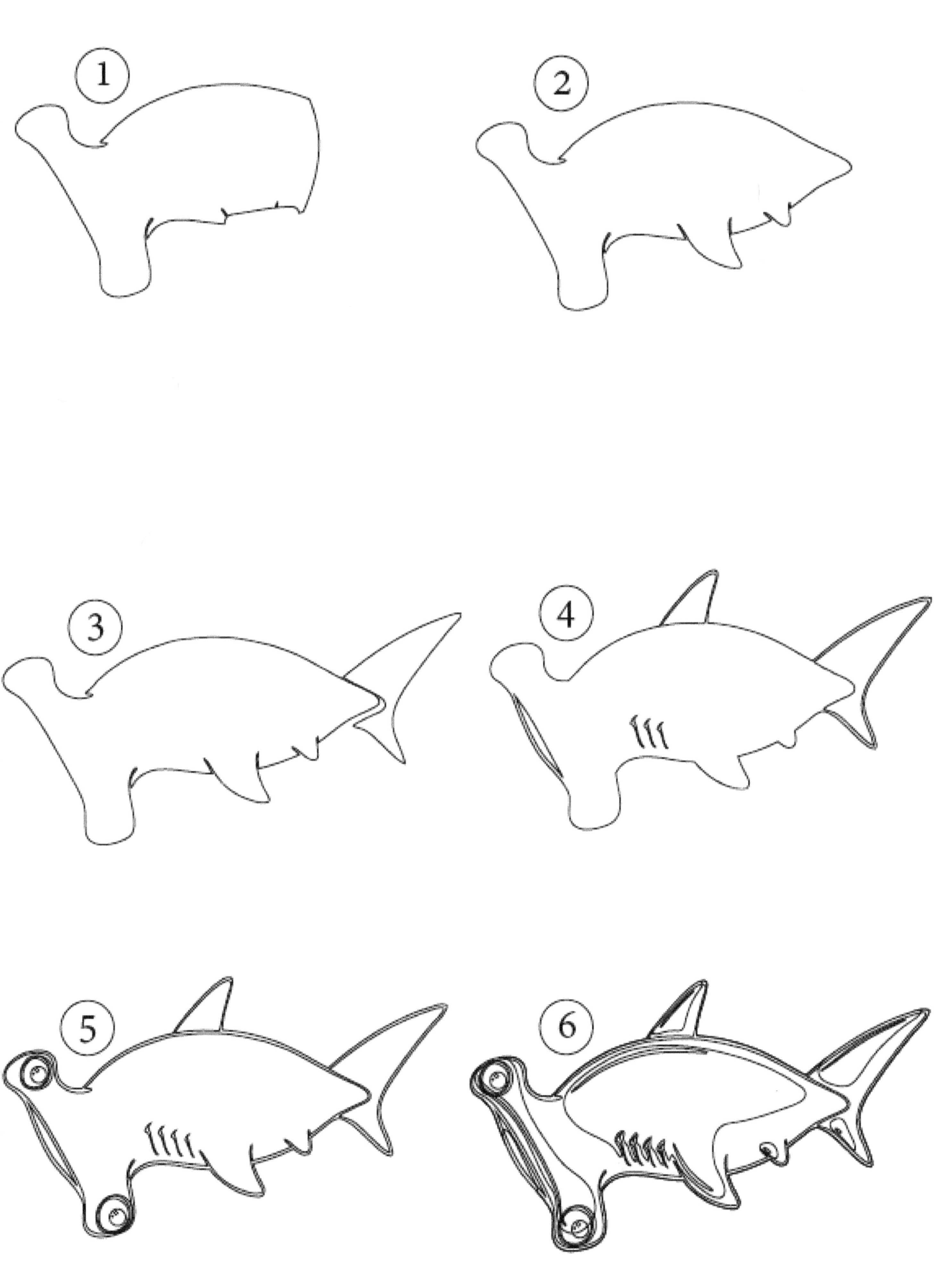

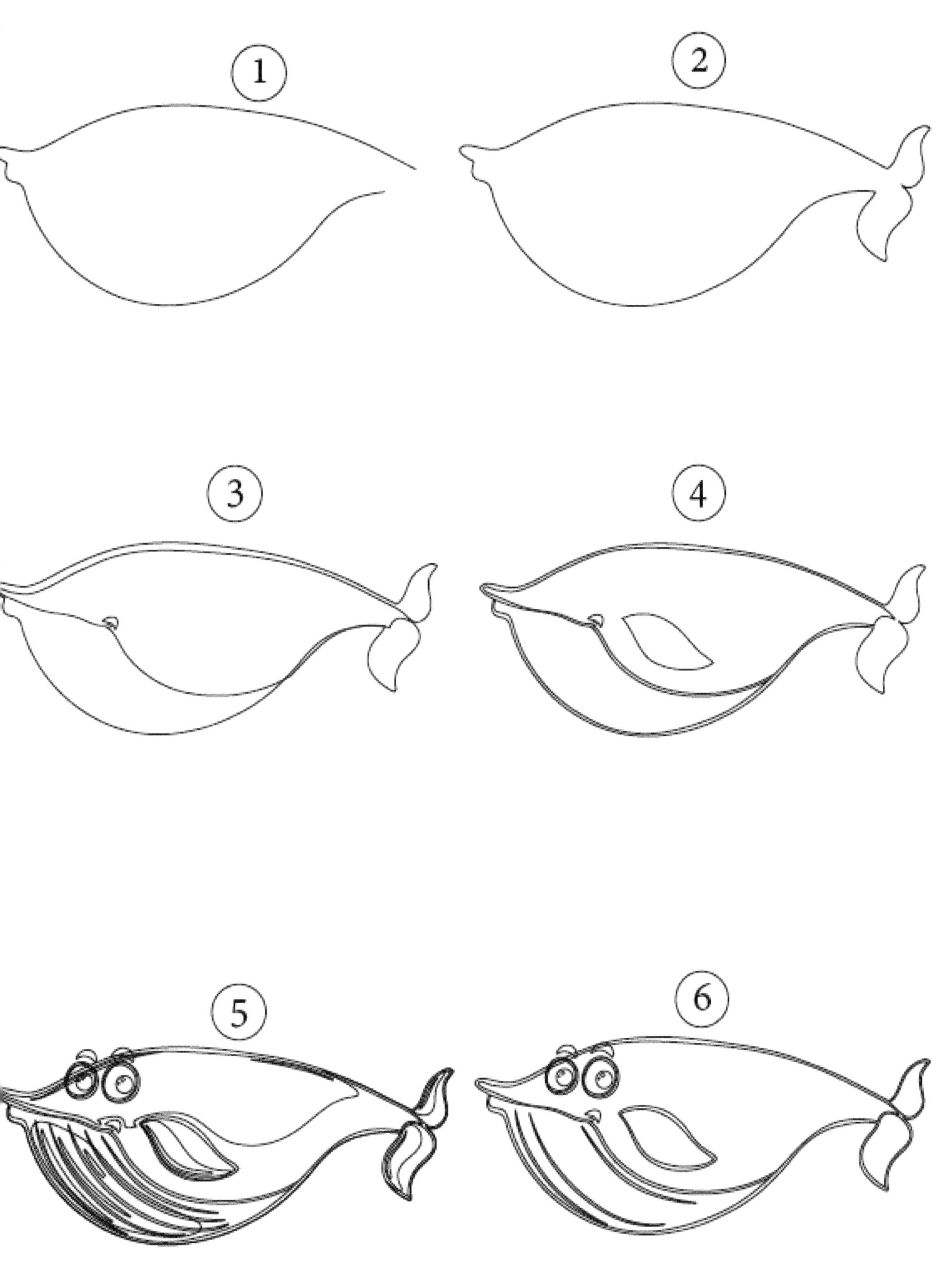

1
2
3
4
5
6

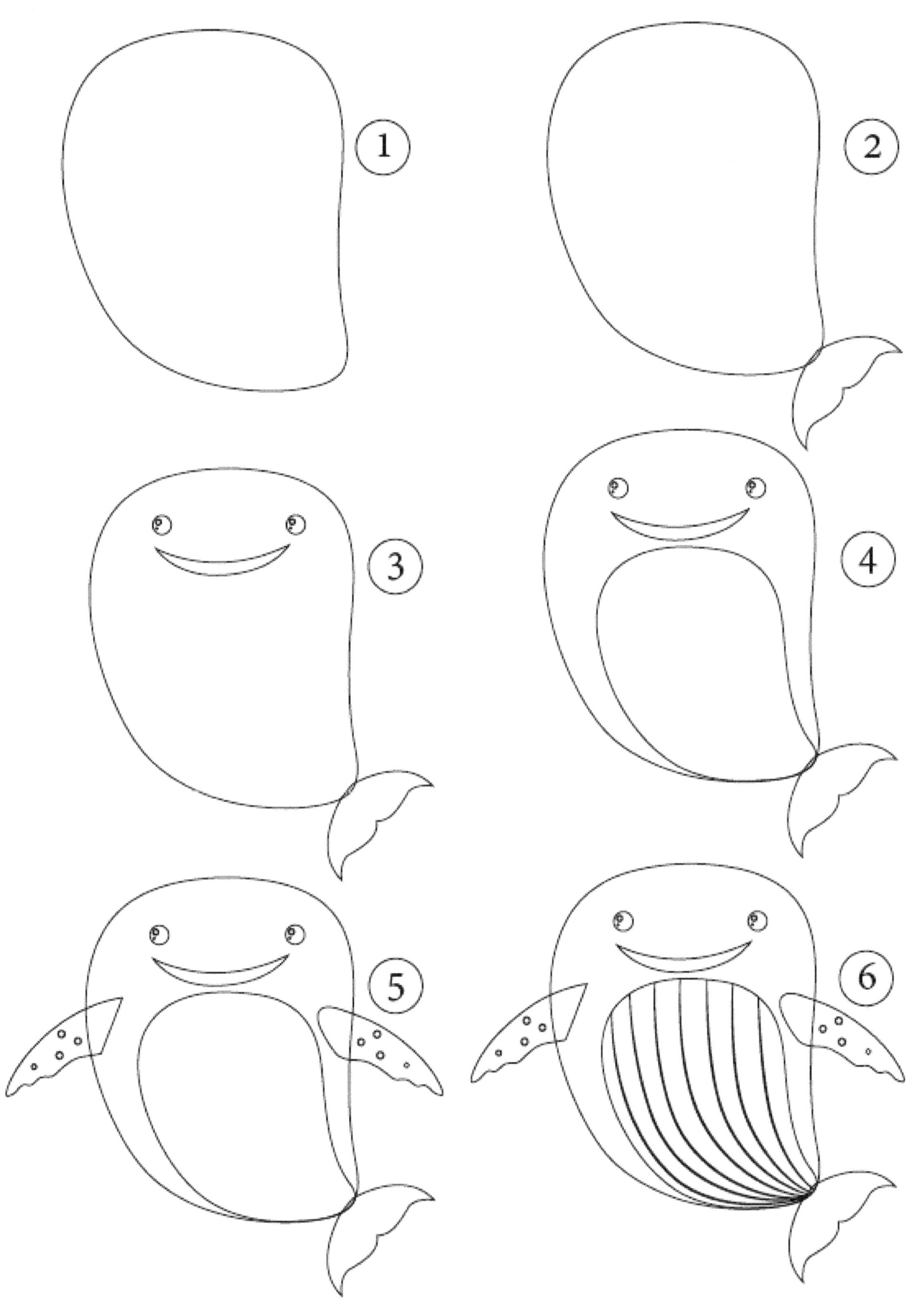

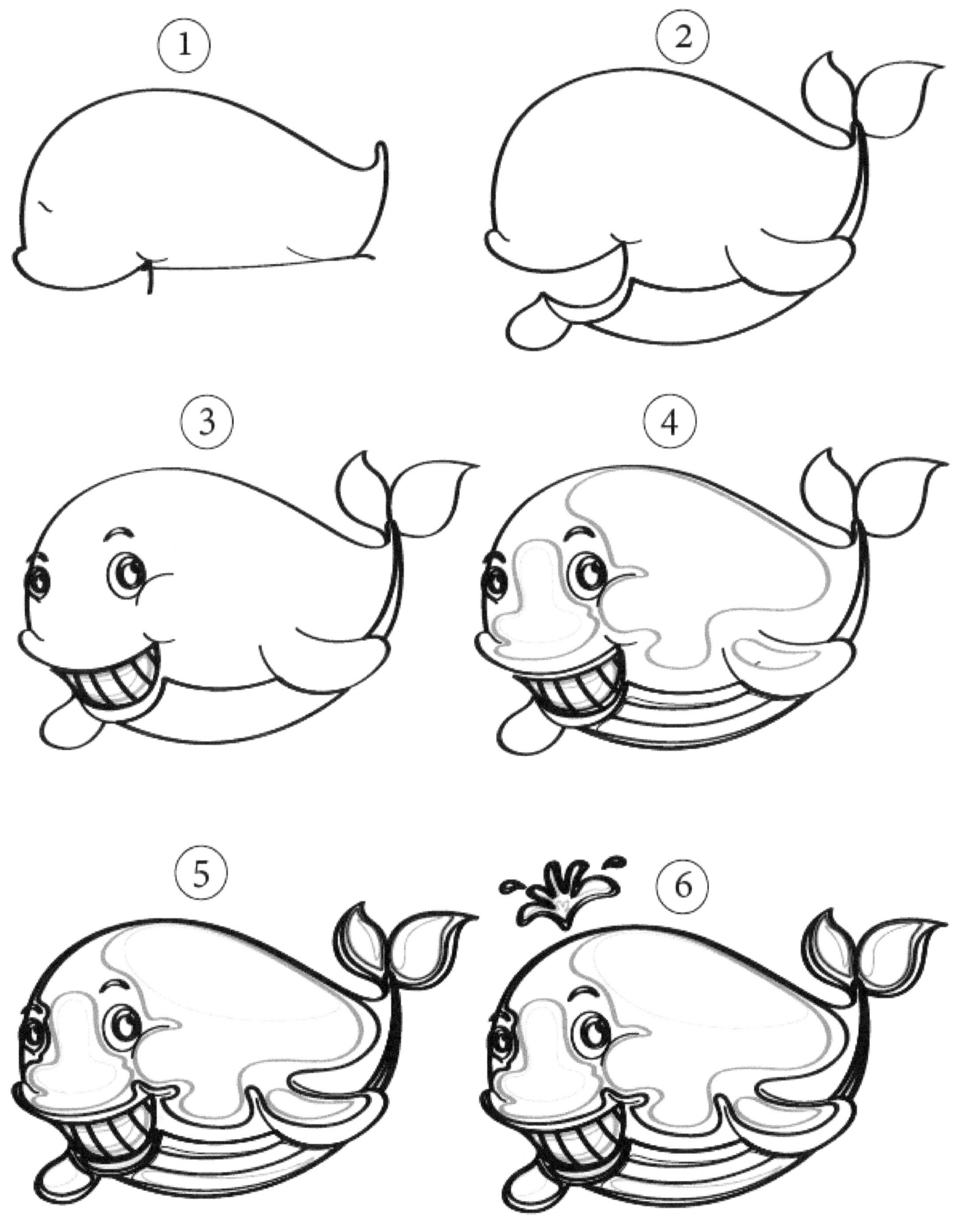

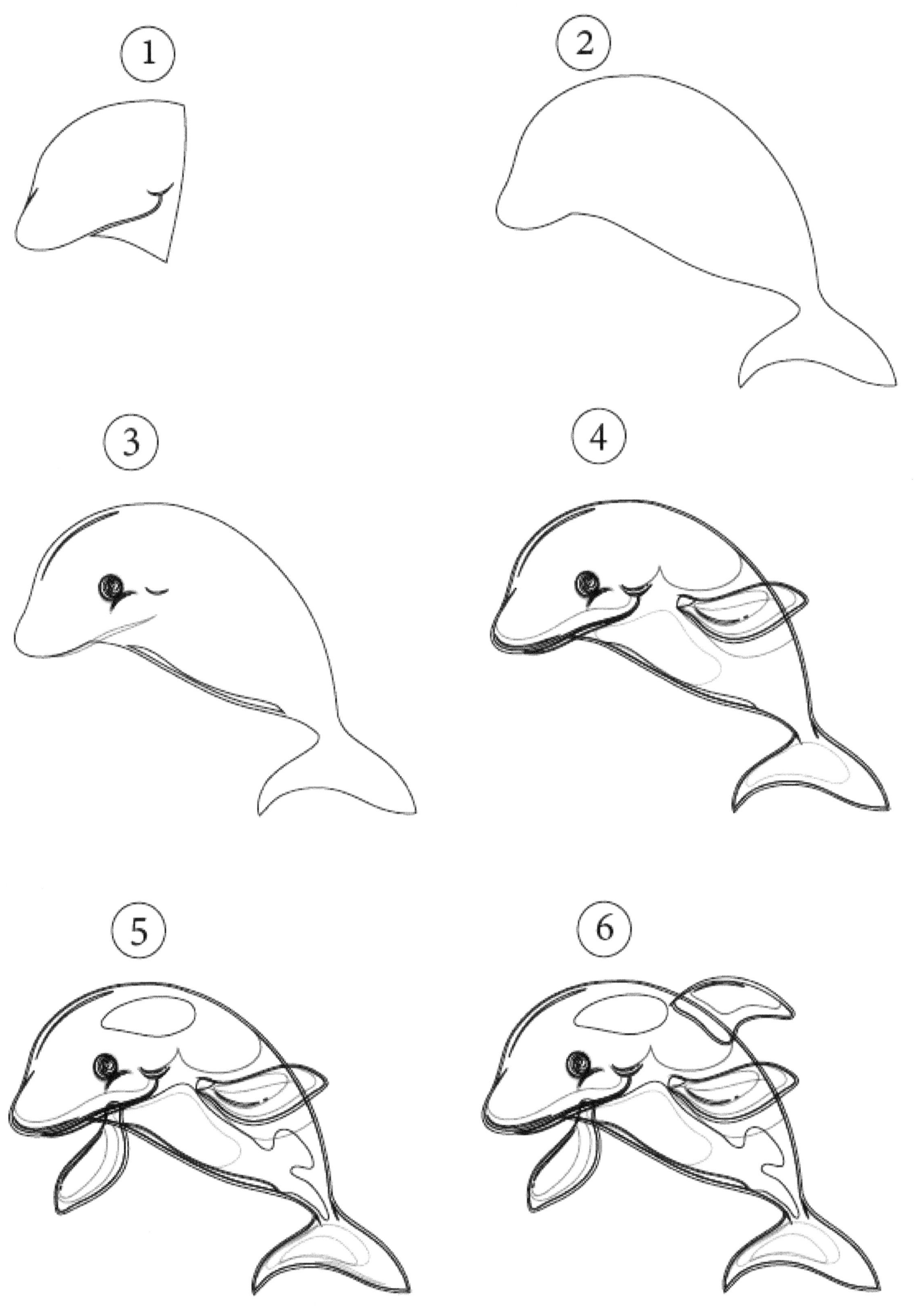

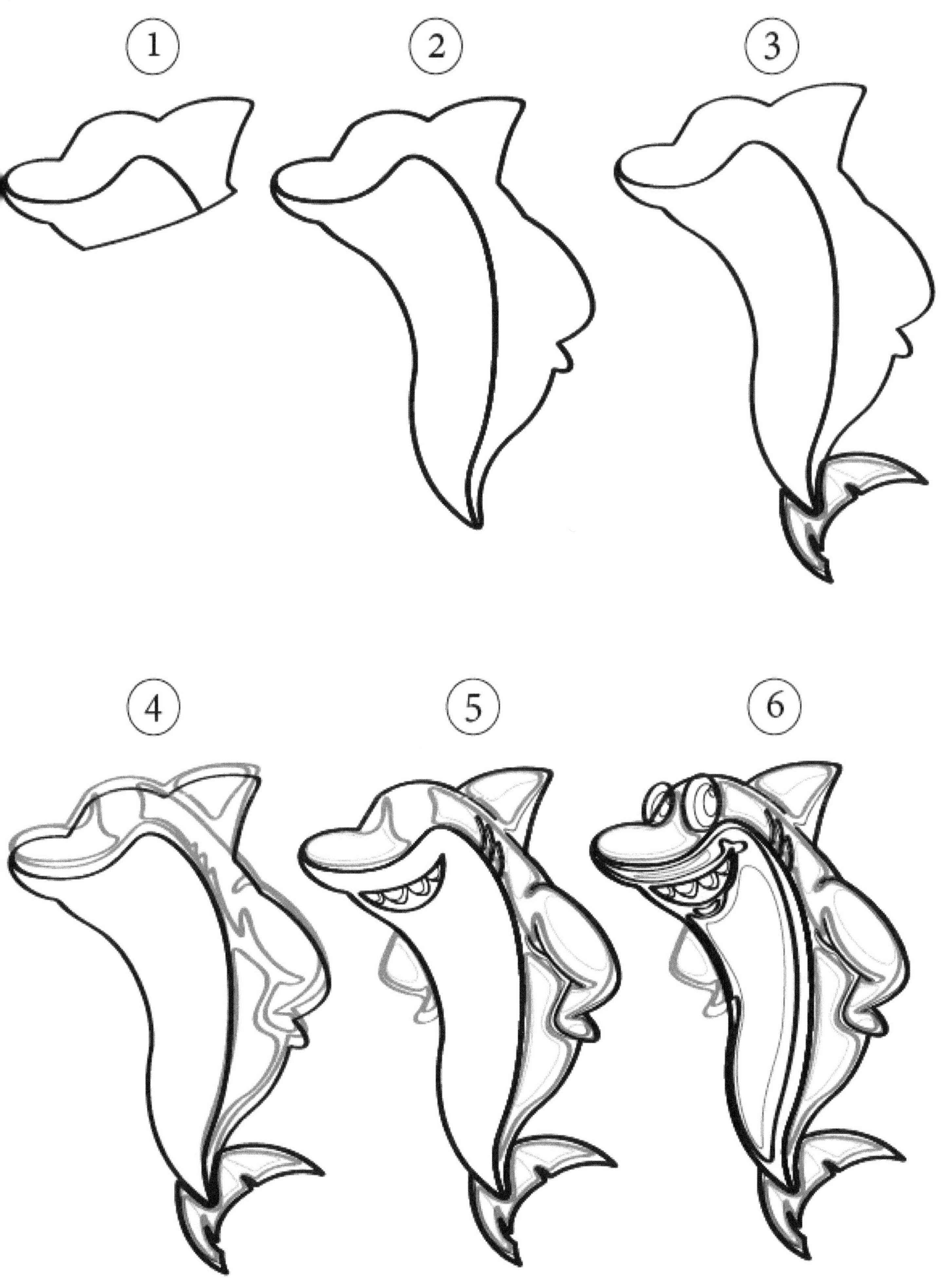

1
2
3
4
5
6

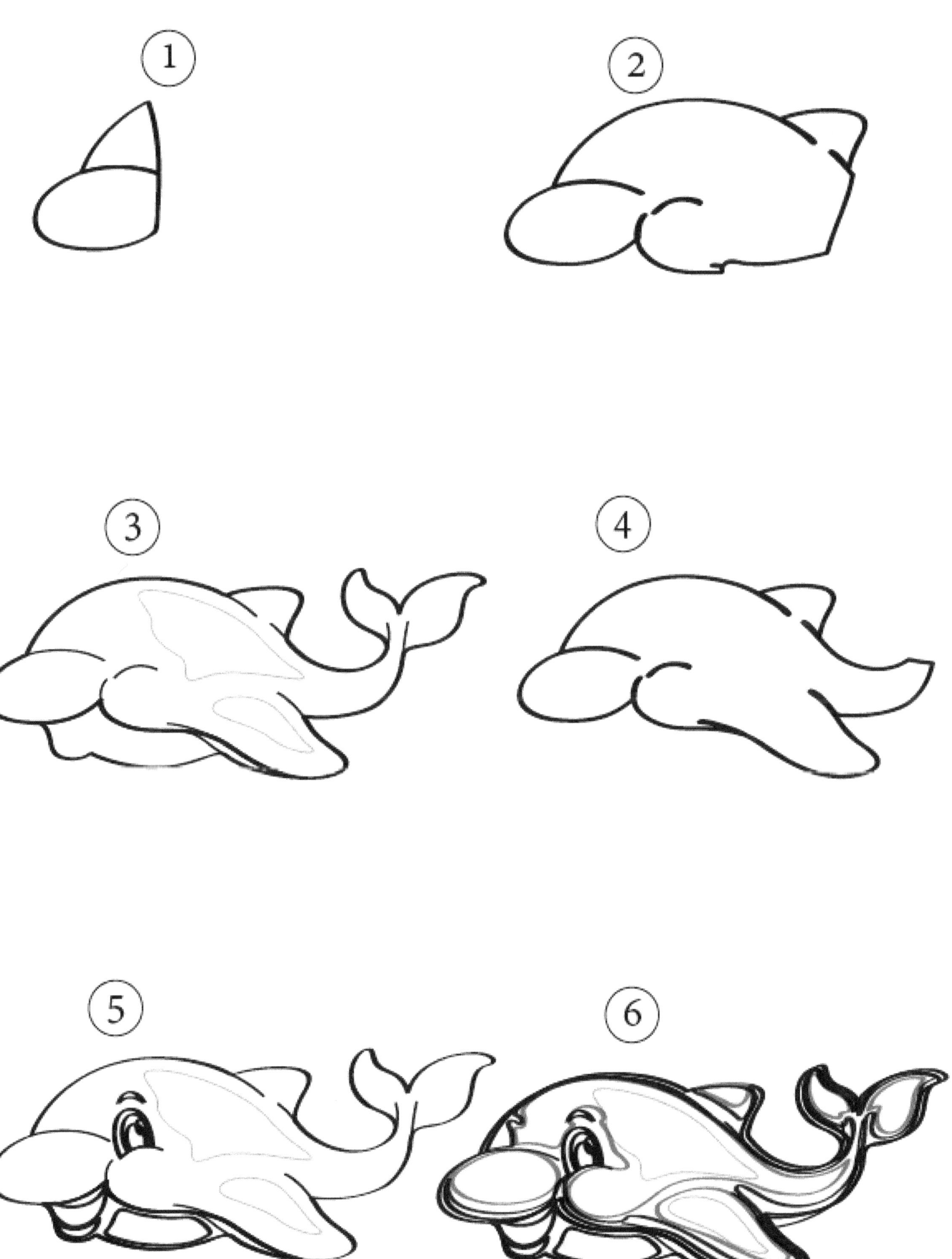

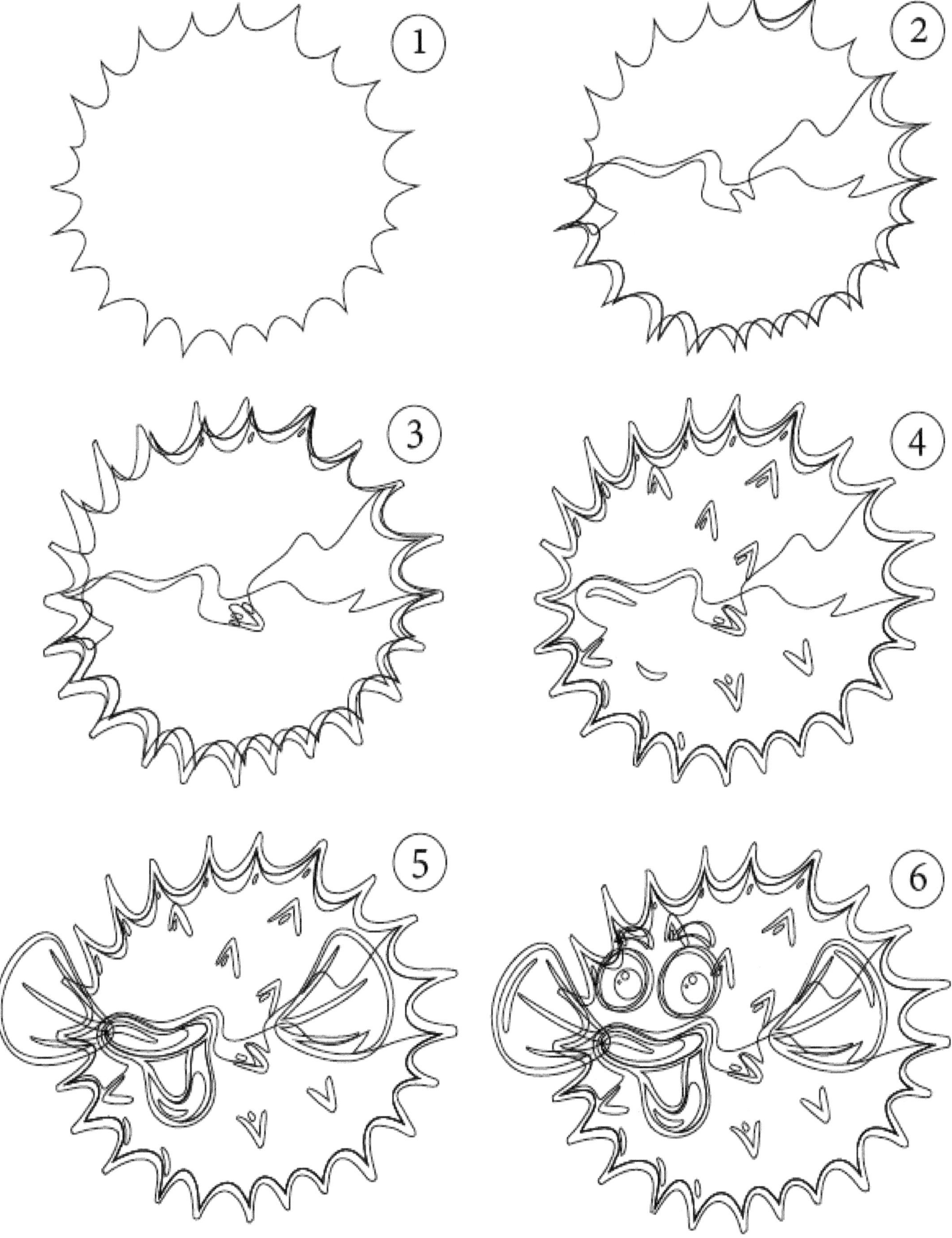

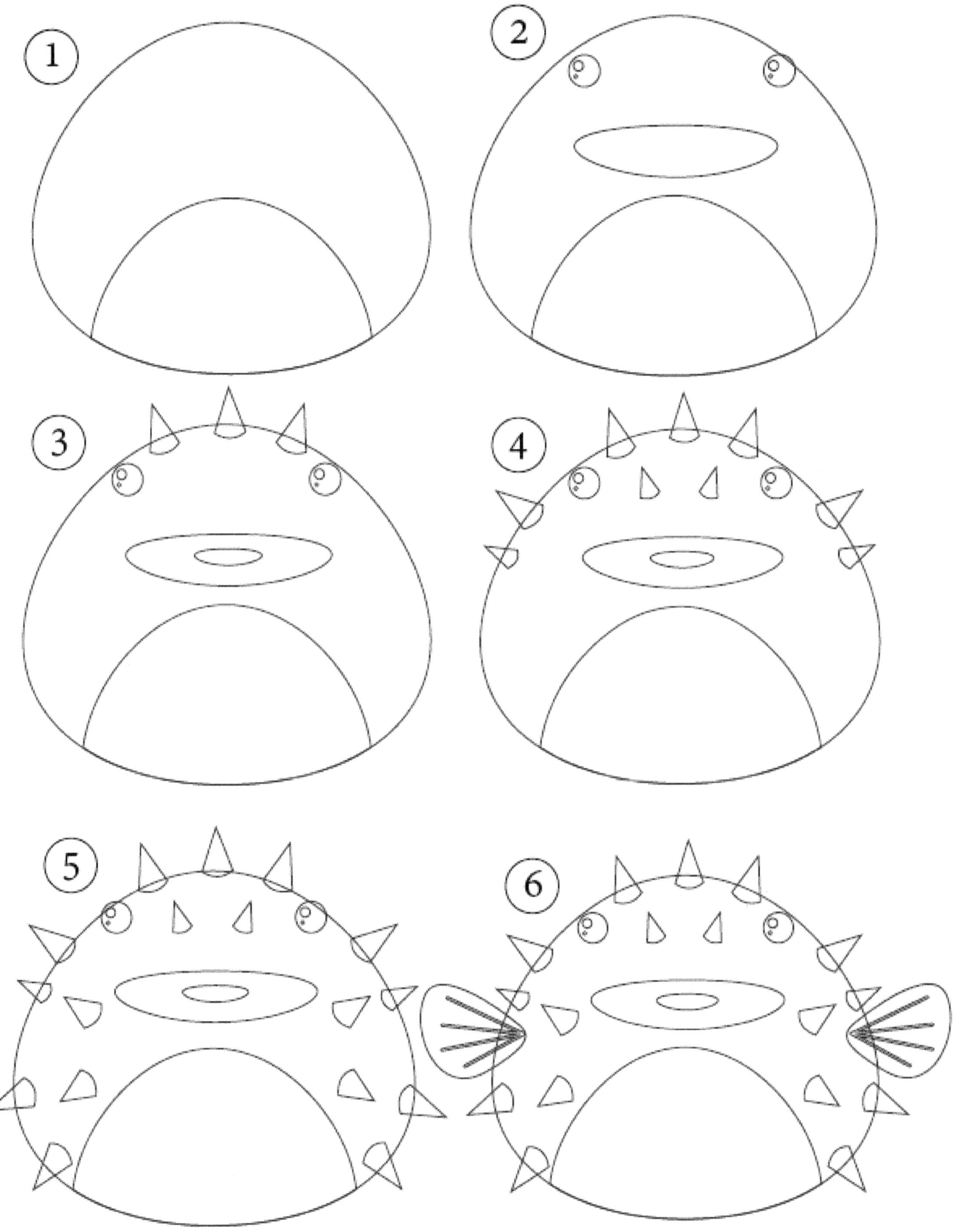

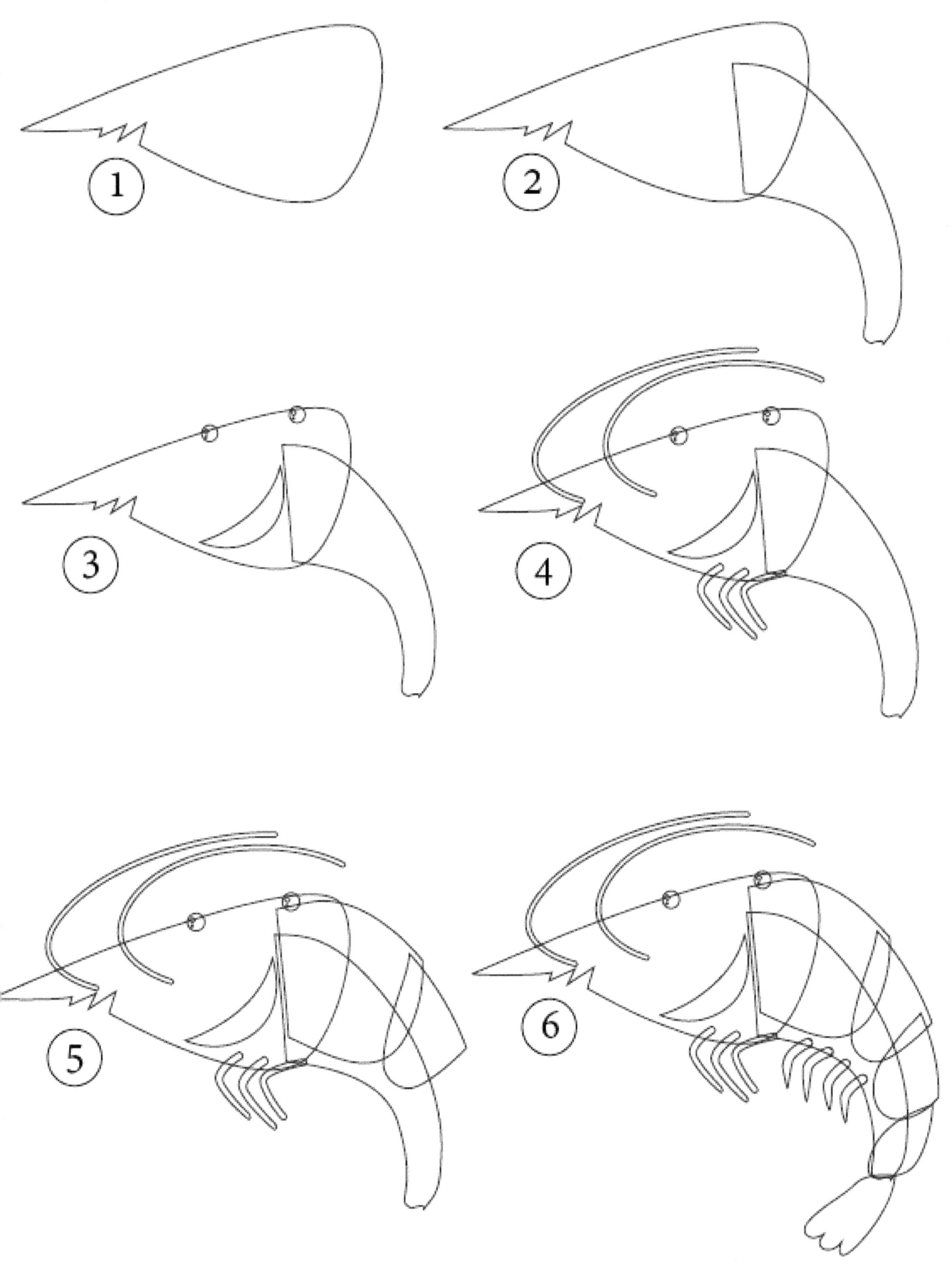

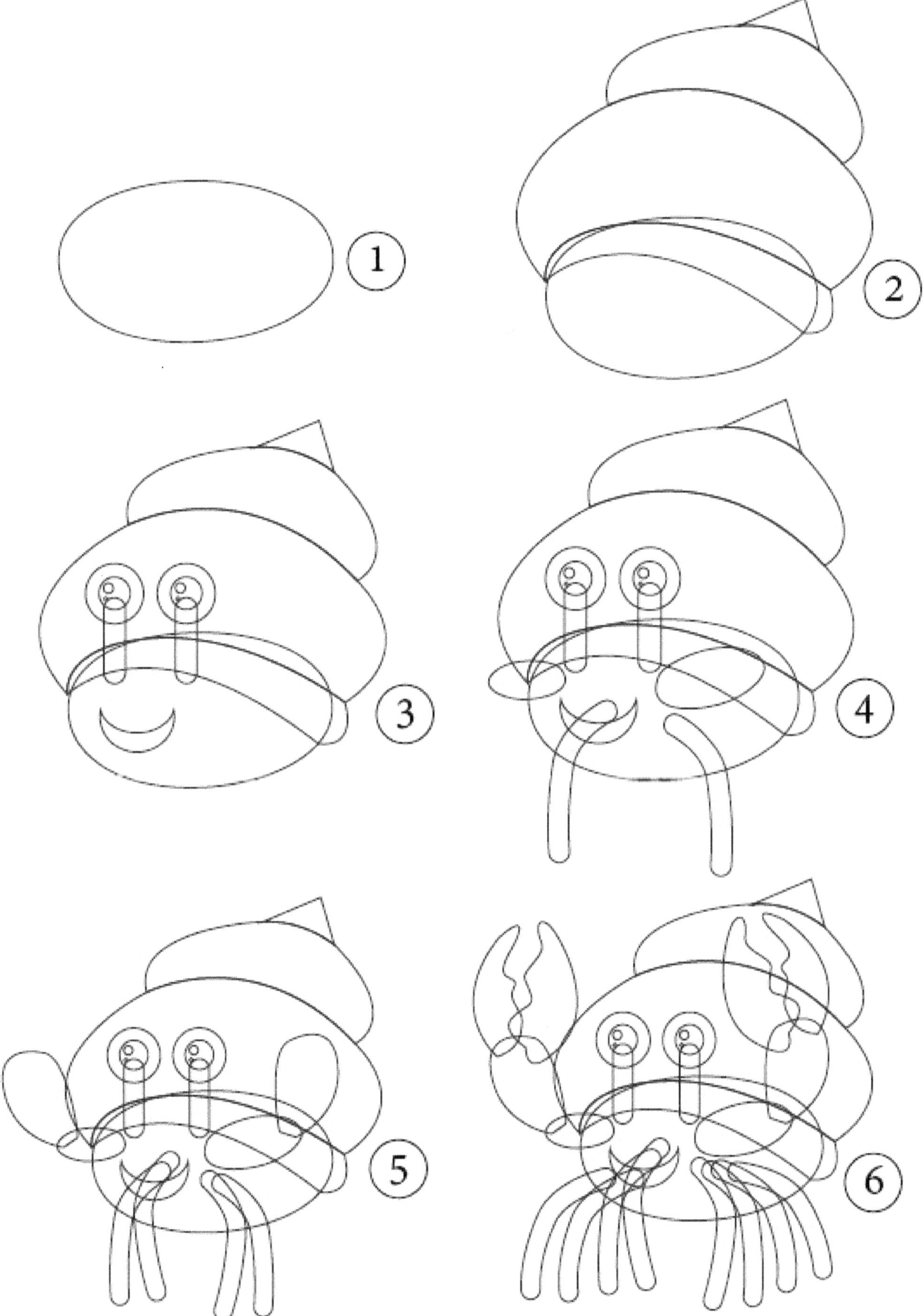
1
2
3
4
5
6

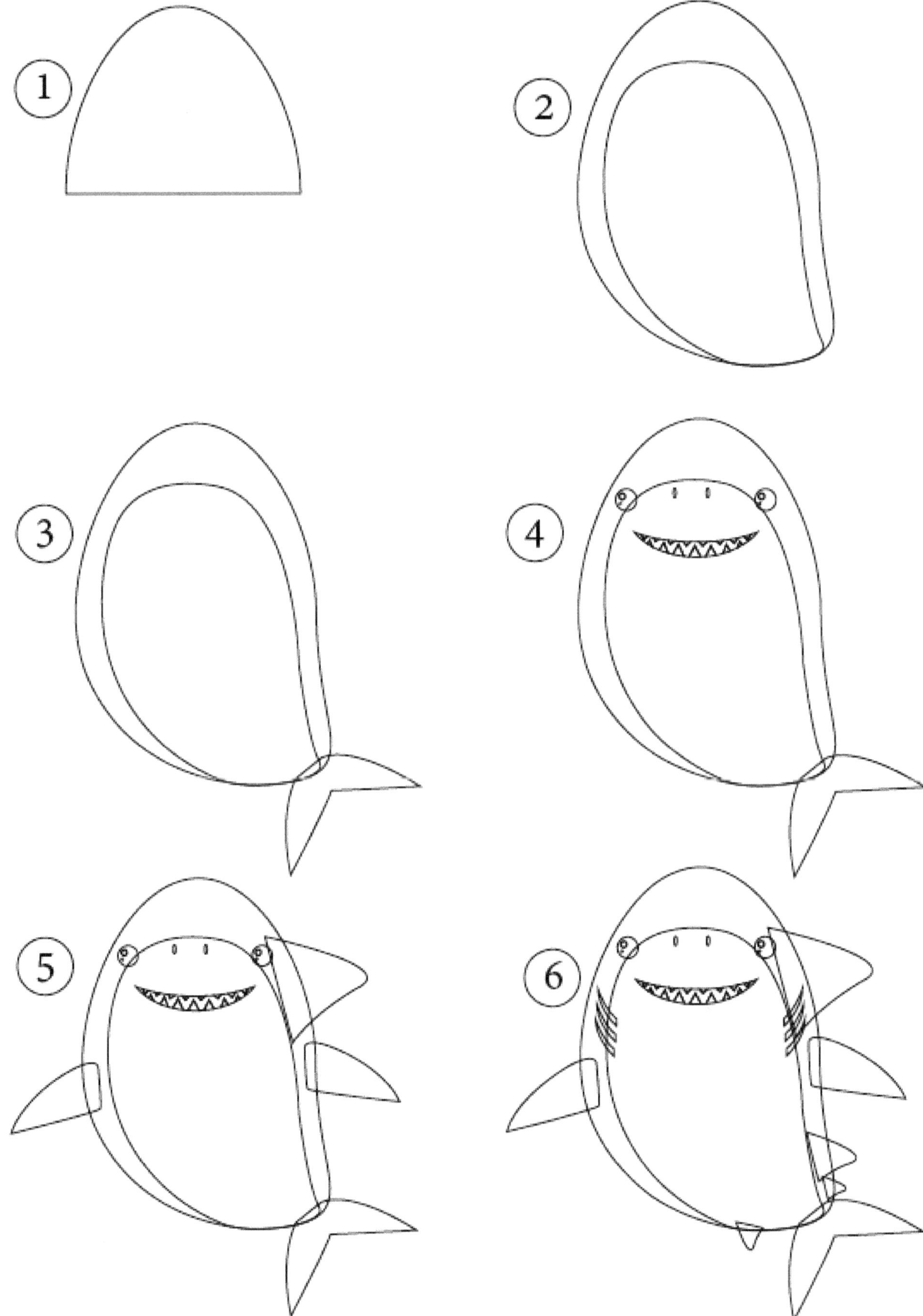